Dead Heat

(Book 3 in the Bluegrass Series)

Kathleen Brooks

Books by Kathleen Brooks

Bluegrass Series

Bluegrass State of Mind

Risky Shot

Dead Heat

Bluegrass Brothers Series

Bluegrass Undercover

Rising Storm

Secret Santa, A Bluegrass Series Novella

Acquiring Trouble

Relentless Pursuit

Secrets Collide

To my husband, daughter, parents, in-laws and friends
who provided me with the encouragement
to follow my passion.

Prologue

Paige Davies sat behind her sales counter and tapped her fingernails on its white top. Betty Jo Simpson was due to start her shift five minutes ago. She let out another agitated sigh as she looked at the clock. Looking around her shop always calmed her. The walls were painted the palest of yellow. She had sewn the blue, white, and yellow curtains and trimmed them in lace. To the right of the open main room, the hat room was painted white to allow the hats to pop. Tables were covered in the same material she had used on the curtains. Decorative ribbon roped off the staircase on the far left of the main room leading to her second-story apartment. The windows let in the bright summer sunlight. She had placed crystal, glass, and jewelry displays along the large front windows to draw customers in with their sparkles. The feel should be light and comfortable, which is what she always felt when she was in her store.

Paige stopped drumming her nails and pulled out a new hair tie she was working on. She had used a plain hairband and sewn a perfect bow made out of ribbon onto it. She had then dunked it in a clear paste that hardened the bow. The result was a cute bow that did not come untied every five minutes. She was hoping they would become the new "must have" for the approaching school year. She also hoped some of the mothers would take a liking to them to dress up their jeans or to wear when they played tennis or went riding.

The one she held in her hands was red and white gingham. She looked down at her cotton and spandex red t-shirt and her jean miniskirt tied off with a red scarf belt she had made and knew this was the perfect bow for it. She reached back with both hands and gathered up her light-brown hair into her right hand. She was going to need her hair cut soon. She liked her hair right around shoulder length, but it was slowly creeping down to her shoulder blades. Using her left hand, she deftly tied her hair back into a ponytail.

Paige turned to the mirror behind the counter to check out her handiwork. The tails of the ribbon hung just right. Not so long as to detract from someone's hair and not so short you couldn't tell it was there. If she got a good response at lunch today, then she would think about putting out a small display for the weekend.

She glanced at the clock again and had to stop herself from groaning. She was supposed to meet Dani and Kenna for lunch and was going to be late if Betty Jo didn't show up soon. As if the silent cursing in her head conjured up her harried teenage help, Betty Jo flounced into the store.

"About time. Your shift started ten minutes ago."

"I am so sorry!" Betty Jo was always so sorry. The *so* being dragged out into three or four syllables just to show you how sorry she really was. Betty Jo Simpson was the current reigning Keeneston High prom queen. She had long blonde hair down to her bra line that somehow always had the perfect amount of curl to it. She was tall, thin, and graced with breasts that made Paige's *B*-cup seem inadequate. For what she lacked in promptness, she did make up for in sales and fashion sense. She had started working for Paige two years ago as part of a co-op program with the school. Betty Jo wanted to run her own boutique of high-end clothes. Paige had jumped at the chance to mentor a student. Plus, she needed the extra part-time help. Now that Betty Jo had graduated and been accepted into the fashion design program at the University of Kentucky, Paige had given her more hours and more responsibility. The only thing she couldn't drill into Betty Jo's head was the importance of time management.

"I am late for lunch with the girls. The deliveryman from the supplier in Tennessee should be here in thirty minutes. The checklist is under the counter. Make him show you everything before you sign the receipt. I don't want to get stuck with more of that God-awful flower fabric again. Don't take anything not on the list." Paige turned and headed for the door. "Be back in an hour!" she waved over her shoulder.

"Ooh! You're wearing the new hair ribbons! I love, love, love it!"

Paige stopped and turned back around with a smile on her face. "Really? Great! Go through our ribbon stock and pick out the colors you think would sell the best for the different age groups. I will start working on them tonight. See you in a bit." Paige waved again as she pulled open the front door. She smiled at the mother-daughter team who walked past her and into the shop, making excited noises as they pointed out items they liked. She felt as if every person who walked into her store was walking into her home, and not just because she lived upstairs. Her store was an extension of her.

Paige took in a deep breath of the humid air. Phew, it was going to be hot. She looked up at the bank sign and saw that not only was she late, but it was also ninety-three degrees outside. As if to tell her "duh!" trickles of sweat rolled down her cheek. She looked across the street and saw some shade if she walked close enough to the buildings. Hey, some shade was better than baking in the hot summer sun. She crossed the street halfway to the cafe as soon as the light held up the lunchtime traffic.

She looked back across the street to the courthouse and saw the first couple of people push out the side door. She was just in time. If she hurried, she could still snag a table from Miss Daisy and not have to wait. She picked up her speed and hurried along past the storefronts displaying antique chests, dining sets, and old artwork. As she hurried past the American flags waving on the streetlights and past the baskets of petunias, marigolds, and ivy lining Main

Street, she kept her eye on the side door. If a wave of people were to come out, then she wasn't above making a dash for the cafe to cut in front of them to secure a table. Sure, they had patio tables with umbrellas outside, but the heat was smothering. No way was she going to sit out there and melt.

Two blocks from the crosswalk at Elm and Main, she saw the side door to the courthouse open. Dani and Kenna pushed their way through. By the huge smile on their faces, it looked like it would be a fun lunch. She saw Kenna point in her direction and waved as Dani made eye contact. Paige pointed to the cafe in an "I'll meet you there" move and saw Kenna nod her head in agreement.

Paige looked back to the cafe to judge whether she needed to break into her version of speed walking to reach the door before the court workers. She picked up her speed and was contemplating a dead run to beat out the county clerk when a bright light caught her eye. It was just a quick flash, but it had come from the roof. Paige squinted and looked up the three-story building to see what could possibly be on the roof reflecting light. She looked again, but it was gone. She was about to give up when she saw a long black barrel come into view. The roof was flat but had a three-foot stone wall encasing it to hide the sight of ugly air-conditioning units and other electrical features. The barrel slowly extended on the rail and stopped. Looking back, she saw a figure rising up from behind the rail.

She followed the angle of the barrel to the courthouse, and in that split second it made sense. This wasn't maintenance, this wasn't a surveyor or even a cameraman. That was a rifle and he was aiming at someone coming out of the courthouse. She opened her mouth and screamed as loud as she could. Her screams of warning were cut off by two loud gunshots. She tried to see who was shot, but the courthouse parking lot was filled with people hiding behind cars, lying on the pavement, and screaming as they ducked for cover. Shouts were coming from people trying to push their way back into the building for safety. Shoppers poured out of the tiny shops up and down Main Street trying to see what was going on.

She looked back up at the roof, but the man was gone. The people at the courthouse were looking all around, but it was obvious they couldn't tell where the shots had come from. Her feet kicked in before her brain did and she took off at a dead run for the cafe.

"What are you doing, Paige?" she asked herself as she ran past the chaos erupting at the courthouse. She was not heroic, that was her brothers' job. But their military instincts rubbed off on her as she raced toward the danger instead of away from it. Her brothers had always said the more dangerous the situation, the calmer they became. She understood what they meant and couldn't tell if that was good or not. The screaming, crying, and shouting faded away. Her vision focused on the cafe as she scanned the roof for traces of the gunman. The only sounds she heard were the pounding of her new white tennis shoes on the sidewalk and the beating of her heart. Out of the corner of her eye she saw Dinky rushing through the large wood front doors of the courthouse.

"Dinky!" she screamed and waved an arm in the air until he saw her. "I saw him. Cafe roof!" she yelled over the noise of mass confusion and pointed to the near side of the cafe. She had to take a gulp air as she swam through the humidity weighing her down. She saw Dinky point to the far side of the building and acknowledged his signal with her own. Dinky would take the far side, she'd take the one closest to her. She tried one more time to see if anyone was hit, but it was still too chaotic. The Sheriff's Department was out in full force trying to get some order by setting up as much a perimeter as three men and two women who worked the phones could do.

Paige cut to her left and headed down Elm Street. The cafe sat on the corner of Main and Elm and ran down Elm for almost a block. Like most buildings from the late 1700s and early 1800s, it was tall, narrow, and deep. There was a small alley that ran behind the building leading to a parking lot that sat behind the Main Street stores and businesses. If he were coming off the roof, he'd probably try to escape from the back of the building and, hopefully, run into either her or Dinky. Pushing hard, she burst through the dark alley and into the parking lot. Her breath came in deep pants as awareness seeped into her body. Awareness that the person she was looking for was an armed, dangerous killer. She started to scan the parking lot for people as she wiped the sweat stinging her eyes from her brow. Her head snapped instantly to her right at the sound of a door being opened.

There he was. The man walked calmly out the kitchen door of the cafe carrying a duffle bag that she presumed held the rife. He was about five ten, brown hair trimmed short, athletic, mid-forties, black suit, white shirt, and no tie. He approached a tan sedan and opened the front door to get in.

"Stop!" Paige didn't know what she would do if he did stop, and she definitely did not know what she would do if he did not stop, but the word tumbled out anyway. At least she didn't follow it up with "or else I'll shoot." The man looked up and her hazel eyes met his brown ones. It felt as if they stared at each other for minutes. The world stopped turning, the sweat stopped running down her face, and noises faded. A split second later, the man broke eye contact and slid into his car. Paige jumped forward as soon as the man got into this car and started it. A blur in brown caught her attention as she quickly glanced toward the far side of the parking lot, past the cafe. With gun drawn, Dinky raced around the side of the building and sprinted toward her, glancing all around the parking lot as he did.

"Tan sedan!" she managed to scream as she willed her feet to move faster. The man floored the gas pedal. The tires screeched as the sedan shot forward. Their eyes locked one more time as he hit the accelerator and drove the car right at her. The look in his eyes left her with no doubt that he would bounce her off the car faster than a flea could wink. Paige hurled her body to the left row of parked cars and landed beside a Chevy pickup truck just as the tan sedan flew by.

"Paige! Paige! You okay?"

"Yeah, did you get anything, Dink?

"Got a plate, but my guess is it will be stolen. But at least it's something." Dinky came to a stop beside the truck and leaned down to help her up.

"Thanks." Paige stood and brushed some loose gravel from her knees and the palms of her hands. They'd need a couple Band-Aids, but nothing too serious. "You know if anyone was hit?"

"Don't know. As soon as I heard the shots I tried to get outside. But people were scared and trying to get back inside. I ended up going out the front door and that's when I heard you. Come on, let's tell Red what we saw and run this plate."

She easily kept up with Dinky's stride as they cut through the cafe's empty kitchen and went through the equally empty dining room. It was the first time Paige had seen the cafe empty and it left her with an eerie, foreboding feeling.

They pushed open the glass door to the cafe and stepped out on the sidewalk across the street from the courthouse. People lined the street and crowded the parking lot. Whispering and speculation ran rampant as people tried to guess what had happened. Dinky and Paige crossed the street and walked through the crowd milling about. They found a tight group of people in a circle formation about halfway across the parking lot and close to the side door. Dinky pushed his way through and Paige stuck to him like glue. Some people were crying, some were looking around, but mostly the large group was quiet. That couldn't be good. The foreboding feeling danced around her, almost laughing. Dinky stopped suddenly and Paige ran into his back.

"What is it, Dinky?"

Dinky didn't answer, just moved out of the way so Paige could see.

"Oh my God."

Chapter One

Paige looked over Dinky's shoulder and into a living nightmare. Two unresponsive bodies lay on the pavement. Red, the sheriff of Keeneston, was kneeling on the ground, focused on giving CPR to Danielle as blood pooled under her. Martha was pressing her blood-covered hands against McKenna's shoulder trying to control the bleeding running down her arm.

Paige looked up as she saw the crowd near the courthouse shift. Henry shoved his way through and dropped to the ground beside Red. Neither looked to each other, neither talked, but they worked as a fluid pair. Henry, the defense attorney who shared office space with Kenna, straddled Dani and started doing chest compressions as Red took over breathing for Danielle. The action kicked Paige out of her trance. She rushed forward, her heart having stopped beating ten minutes ago and she was pretty sure it wouldn't start again for quite a long time.

She knelt down on the hot pavement beside Dani and pressed her hand against the wound on her chest. If she could stop the bleeding like Martha was doing, maybe Dani would have a chance. There was just so much blood. Blood seeped between her fingers and flowed down her arm. It wasn't working. She looked around for something to press against the gunshot wound. She untied the red silk scarf she was using as a belt and pressed it into the wound. She pressed with all her strength and willed the blood to stop flowing.

"Someone call an ambulance!" she yelled into the faceless crowd.

"The ambulances are on their way from Lexington. They'll be here in another fifteen minutes." Noodle yelled back as he rushed from the courthouse with an emergency first-aid kit.

"To hell with the ambulances! Tell them to send the helicopter. I don't know how much longer she'll hold on," Red shouted before breathing into Danielle's mouth again. Henry was counting 1-2-3-4-5 as he compressed her chest over and over again, sweat running down his white face.

"Already did. Heli's three minutes out." Noodle shouted over the noise of the crowd as he handed the first-aid kit to Judge Cooper who was still in his black robe. "Come on, people, get back! Get back! We gotta land a helicopter here." Noodle started shoving people out of the parking lot. "Come on, Dinky, get those people out of here!"

"Paige. Paige! Take this and try to stop the bleeding." Judge Cooper shoved a packet of powdered coagulant into her shoulder until she grabbed it. Oh God, what was she doing? What was happening? She shook her head. She didn't have the time to break down. Not when her friends' lives depended on people keeping calm. She ripped the package open and poured it into Dani's wound. Judge Cooper shoved some gauze into her hand. She replaced her scarf with the gauze and immediately wished she hadn't. Her red scarf didn't show how much Dani was bleeding. The white gauze turned red at an alarming rate. She pushed harder and hoped the powder would work. She wanted to ask for another gauze, but Judge Cooper had already turned to help Martha with Kenna's head wound as she worked on the bleeding coming from the shoulder wound.

"Move! Get out of our way!" Paige looked up in time to see a broom come down over the head of a man blocking the way of the three Rose sisters. "We got blankets and clean cloths," Miss Lily yelled as she cleared a path through the crowd with her broom, her two sisters following closely behind.

"Dani's unconscious and isn't breathing!" Paige yelled to them as they made their way forward.

"Kenna is unconscious; a bullet went through her shoulder and there's a bump on her head." Judge Cooper shouted over his shoulder as he dug around the first-aid kit looking for more gauze. "We need more strips to slow the bleeding over here!"

"Here you go." The Rose sisters branched out and took command as if they were generals on the battlefield.

Miss Lily, armed with a stack of cloths, went to help Judge Cooper and Martha. Miss Violet laid a blanket over Dani's bare legs and Miss Daisy placed her hands over Paige's. Paige looked up at the quiet confidence that hung on every move the sisters made. They worked silently and quickly. More strips of cloths were set next to her, blankets appeared, and encouraging touches were given. They somehow seemed to know what she needed even before she did.

Paige took a quick look around. Henry was still straddling Dani, administering chest compressions. Blood, dirt, and sweat covered his face. The cuffs of his white dress shirt were stained red with blood. Red was flushed, sweat running down his cheeks and disappearing under the collar of his brown uniform as he breathed for Dani. Paige looked down at her own hands covered in her friend's blood and pressed hard against Dani's chest. Miss Daisy's wrinkled but steady hands appeared with a new cloth to replace the bloody one.

Paige lifted her hands allowing Miss Daisy to remove the gauze and lay on the new cloth. There was blood, so much blood. Her two friends lay unconscious. This couldn't be happening, what was happening? She felt numb. She felt as if she wanted to scream and cry at the same time. She wanted to force herself to wake from this living, breathing nightmare.

"Paige. It's okay, dearie. I got this if you need a break." She looked down at her shaking hands when she felt the squeeze. Miss Daisy had sat down next to her on the rough, blood-soaked pavement and was looking her in the eyes. It took a second, but her mind finally realized Miss Daisy was letting her know she could take over if Paige wanted. But she couldn't. She couldn't give up on her best friends. They would never give up on her.

"Thanks, Miss Daisy, I'm okay now."

"Just focus on what's right in front of you and leave everything else until later. You know, think like a guy." Miss Daisy gave her a wink and a quick reassuring squeeze.

Paige pressed the cloth to the wound and was relieved when it wasn't instantly drenched in Dani's blood like the gauze had been.

"Everyone back! Make room, the heli's landing." Noodle yelled as he and Dinky pushed the crowd back some more.

Paige looked up into the sky and saw the helicopter off in the distance. "Thank God."

"Amen." Henry and Red said at the same time before going back to CPR.

"Here, cover them the best you can so the wound stays clean when the helicopter lands." Miss Violet passed out the blankets to cover Danielle and Kenna as the helicopter started to circle and land where Noodle stood directing it on Main Street.

The side door opened and two paramedics jumped out, pulling a board with them. Relief washed over Paige along with a sense of such urgency she thought her heart would burst.

"Here! Over here, she's the worse off," Paige waved them over.

"What do we got?"

"Danielle De Luca. She's twenty-seven. Gunshot to the chest. She went down and her breathing has been shallow to nonexistent. We've been administering CPR for four minutes. Got the bleeding slowed with coagulant powder. She's critical." Red shouted over the noise of the helicopter.

"This is McKenna Mason, gunshot to the shoulder. Through and through. Age twenty-nine. Took a bump to her head when she fell. Unconscious, but stable," Judge Cooper informed the paramedic.

"Okay. We'll take this one," he pointed to Dani. "Ambulance will be here shortly to take the other to UK." Paige felt strong hands on her shoulder as she was pulled away from Danielle.

She looked back and saw Miss Violet. Paige stood and collapsed into her strength.

"You did real well, Paige. Real well." Miss Violet stroked her hair and hugged her tight as Dani was loaded into the helicopter. She squinted through the wind from the blades and looked through the window on the side of the helicopter. She saw the men resume CPR as the helicopter lifted into the air and prayed it was enough to keep Dani alive.

Paige looked back at Miss Lily and Martha working together to keep Kenna comfortable. Patting down her pockets, she felt her cell phone in her back pocket and dug it out. She stared at her small black phone in her bloody hands. Shaking her head to clear it, she dialed the number she knew by heart.

"Hey, Paige. What's up?"

"Will. Kenna's been shot." Paige tried to sound calm and steady, but her body wouldn't stop shaking.

"What?" She heard the panic in his voice and tried to stop the tears.

"Kenna and Dani have been shot. Kenna is unconscious but stable. They will be taking her to the University of Kentucky shortly. Dani's been medevacked out."

"I don't understand."

"Kenna was leaving the courthouse and was shot. The ambulance is due here in minutes and we'll be off to the ER at UK."

"I'll meet you there."

Paige pressed the End button and took a deep breath. Miss Violet pressed a clean cloth in her hand.

"It has to be done. He should hear it from a friend, not some emergency personnel. Wipe your face and hands. Take a deep breath and just do it."

"I know. How do I tell someone that I don't know if the love of his life is going to be alive or not by the time he reaches the hospital?"

"You just tell him the facts and then be there for him." Miss Violet patted her hand and walked away.

Paige scrolled down her numbers and hit the call button.

"Hello."

"This is Paige Davies. I have an emergency and I need to speak to the sheik."

"I am sorry, he's in a meeting. Can I take a message?"

"No, you can't take a message. This is an emergency! Interrupt the damn meeting."

"I am sorry, Miss..."

"His fiancé was shot. Do you want to tell him that?"

"Miss Danielle? I'll get him immediately." Paige let out a shaky breath and tapped her foot while she waited.

"Paige? What's wrong?"

"Mo." Her voice cracked and she took a deep breath to regain control of the tears threatening to spill over. Focus on what's in front of you, she told herself. "Dani has been shot in the chest. Her breathing was shallow and sometimes we couldn't detect it. Henry and Red administered CPR. I tried to slow the bleeding the best I could. She was just evacuated on the helicopter. She should be at the UK trauma center in minutes."

She paused, but heard nothing. "Mo? Mo?" She waited again, but didn't hear anything but the sound of shouts in the background and running feet.

Paige hit the End button and scrolled for one more number. She heard the wail of the sirens off in the distance and she pushed the Call button.

"Cole, Kenna and Dani have been shot. Dani was evacuated by helicopter and the ambulance is just now pulling up for Kenna." It felt surreal. She watched the ambulance pull into the parking lot and the doors open. It couldn't be real. This had to be a nightmare.

"Where are they taking them?"

"UK."

"I'll meet you there."

The EMTs loaded Kenna onto a stretcher and rolled her quickly to the ambulance. Paige followed behind them and climbed into the back. She looked back one more time at the crowd gathered. Red was issuing orders. Henry's shiny suit was covered in blood and dirt. His blood-stained hands hung at his sides as he stared absent-mindedly at the ambulance. Martha's white blouse was covered in Kenna's blood. Her normally tight bun had fallen loose around her pale face. The Rose sisters, united as ever, stood side by side as they watched the ambulance doors close.

Chapter Two

Paige sat back and watched the two EMTs work on Kenna. She was still heavily dazed but had started to mumble and tried to move. The EMTs stabilized her arm and wrapped gauze around her head to stop the bleeding from the wound on the back of her head.

The fifteen-minute drive seemed to take an eternity. A fog seemed to settle into Paige's head as she relived the whole event. The sound of the gunfire, the stare-down with the assassin, the blood, and chaos... it was all too much to grasp.

She closed her eyes and listened to the EMTs calling into the ER with their estimated time of arrival. They gave updates on Kenna's condition and took her vitals. Paige let the sounds wash over her as she prayed for her friends.

The ambulance wove its way through the Lexington traffic. Luckily, the campus was pretty empty with it being summer and they managed to avoid any holdups. They pulled under the red emergency sign designating the entrance and came to a stop. The back doors were opened and a score of emergency personnel all dressed in various colored scrubs met them. Kenna was lifted down and wheeled into the ER.

Paige stepped down and was met by an ER nurse in cheery teddy bear scrubs who started peppering her with questions.

"What's her name?"

"McKenna Mason Ashton."

"Is she allergic to anything?"

"I don't know. She never mentioned anything."

"How old?"

"Twenty-nine."

"Married?"

"Yes, her husband is on his way."

"Know her blood type by any chance?"

"Sorry." Paige followed her through the whooshing automatic door and into the lobby of the ER.

"It's okay. We'll take a quick blood test. Is there anything else you know that we should be aware of?"

"No, I don't think so." They stopped at a set of double doors leading back to the emergency room. The nurse hit the button and the doors opened. Paige took a step forward and was stopped.

"Wait here, ma'am. We'll take care of her," the nurse told her as she held up her hands to stop Paige from walking through the doors.

"Before you go, how is Danielle De Luca?" At the nurse's confused expression, she added, "The woman who arrived via helicopter about fifteen minutes ago."

"All I know is that she's in surgery." The nurse turned and rushed through the double doors issuing orders to the other nurses at the station.

Paige was left standing alone, staring at the No Admittance sign. She felt so helpless. Her two best friends were fighting for their lives and she couldn't do anything more to help. She didn't even know if Kenna was allergic to anything. If only she knew what was going on behind those doors. If she could just do something more. Had she done enough to save Dani? She felt the tears stream down her face but was powerless to stop them. She couldn't move her eyes from the double doors.

She felt warm arms wrap around her from behind, pulling her tight against a hard strong body. She lifted her hands up and clasped the anchoring arms as if they were a life preserver. She looked down to see her dirty, bloody hands clinging to the tanned forearm. The sleeves to his black button-up shirt were rolled to his elbows. She clung to him, finding strength in his presence. She didn't need to look around to know who it was. She had known it was him the second he had touched her. Even if his touch hadn't turned her to mush, she just had an innate ability to know when he was near.

"I will fix this. I promise. I will find who did this," Cole whispered into her ear as he pulled her against him.

"I know who did this."

Cole turned her in his arms but kept her pressed against his chest. His hands came up to her dirty face, gently wiping the silent stream of tears away.

"What do you mean you know who did this?" he quietly asked, his silver eyes boring into her hazel ones. He moved his hands to his denim-clad waist in a clear fighting stance. Paige sighed. She didn't want to fight, especially right now, but she couldn't help it. He just couldn't stop acting like an overbearing jerk who had the right to tell her what to do. She just got the feeling she never lived up to his expectations. That she was constantly disappointing him and it caused her to get a little snippy with him sometimes. Okay, most of the time.

"I saw him. His scope caught the sunlight as I was walking to the cafe to meet Dani and Kenna. I saw him pull the trigger. I didn't know who was hit, though. I just took off after him. He was forty-ish, five-ten, light brown hair cut short, and driving a tan sedan. Brown eyes, no visible tattoos."

"How do you know this?"

"Dinky and I chased him off the roof of Miss Daisy's. We found him in the parking lot behind the Main Street stores."

"Did he see you?"

"Of course he did. I just told you I chased him," she snapped.

"How well did he see you?" She saw his jaw tighten but couldn't stop herself.

"Pretty damn well when he almost ran me over with his car. By the way, Dinky was able to get the plate." She felt his hands tighten on her upper arms. He didn't hurt her, actually, she bet he didn't even realize he was doing it. He was just trying to keep his temper under control. She couldn't help herself, though. She had to push him further. She had to get mad. If she got mad, she'd forget about all the pain she had just witnessed. "Did I forget to mention that was after I yelled at him?"

"Dammit, Paige! What are you trying to do, get yourself killed? You go running after a man you know to be armed and dangerous and then you yell at him? That's it, let's go." He grabbed her arm and pulled her toward him as if she were a perp being escorted into jail.

"Go where?" She dug in her heels and yanked her arm out of his grasp.

"Protective custody, that's where." He reached for her again and she stepped back out of his reach.

"I don't think so." Before she could really get going on exactly what she thought of protective custody, the sliding glass entrance doors opened and Mo hurried through. He scanned the room as he moved with the look of a man who owned the hospital. The wrinkled suit and drawn face gave him away, though. His eyes found hers and he lengthened his stride to reach her faster.

"Where is she? Is she alright?" He grabbed her hand and held on for dear life. New tears threatened to spill down her face, but she had to stay strong. Mo and Will would need her to be strong. They would need her to tell them what happened and how the women they loved were doing.

"I don't know. All that the nurse said was she was in surgery. She was shot in the chest. There was a lot of bleeding. Her breathing was very shallow. Red and Henry administered CPR as I tried to stop the bleeding." Paige pulled away from Cole and took his other hand in hers, giving it a squeeze of support. He was so stoic, but if the tense lines etching his face were any indication, he was about to crack soon. She wrapped him in a tight hug and felt him cling to her.

"She's strong, Mo. She'll pull through. She has a wedding to plan, after all. That's enough motivation to pull any woman through."

"I'll tell the nurse you're here and see if there are any more updates," Cole said quietly as he slipped away to the nurses' station.

"I just don't understand what happened. Who shot her?"

"I don't know. I just don't know." Paige wrapped him in another hug and felt him fight the various emotions churning inside of him.

She didn't know how long they stood there, but Paige looked up and over Mo's shoulder when she heard the emergency room door slide open. Will came rushing through the door. His dark brown hair hidden under a blue University of Kentucky hat, his plain white t-shirt covered in sweat, dirt, and hay. It was clear he had rushed straight from the fields to get here. His face had no color, and his brown eyes were filled with worry as he looked at her. She smiled and saw him breathe again.

"Is she okay?"

"Yes, at least I think so. She was unconscious in the ambulance but showed signs of coming around. The bullet went through her right shoulder. The EMTs said she was stable."

"How did this happen?" Will snapped at Cole. Mo's amber gaze aimed at Cole was cold enough to freeze mere mortals.

"I will take the full blame and responsibility for this, and even let you two beat the crap out of me if it makes you feel better. I know you are worried about Danielle and Kenna, and I swear I will find the man who did this. But I have to get Paige out of here. She is in serious danger." Cole ran his large hand through his black hair in a move Paige had come to recognize as meaning he was stressed and agitated.

"Why would Paige be in danger?" Mo sneered at him as if he was an idiot.

"Because she is the only person who can identify the shooter. She not only saw him but also chased him down and yelled at him. If that's not bad enough, they locked eyes so he knows she can identify him. I need to get her into protective custody and in front of a sketch artist right now." Cole wrapped his hand around her upper arm and tried to pull her up against his side again.

"I don't think so, Parker. You want a sketch artist, you bring him here. I am not leaving this hospital." Paige smacked his hand away and imitated Cole's stance by shoving her balled-up fists onto her hips and staring him down. She had five brothers; nothing could intimidate her.

"Fine. I will just arrest you." He reached behind him and pulled out a pair of cuffs.

"For what?" Paige laughed.

"I'll get a material witness order and force you into protective custody." Cole leaned forward, their noses almost touching. Paige just rolled her eyes.

"You know Cade can make those disappear as fast as you can have a judge sign them. Get this through your thick skull, Parker, I am not leaving my friends."

Paige saw Cole's eyes snap to the door behind her. Oh God, please let my friends be alright. She took a deep breath to steady herself for the news and turned to find a shorter man in blue scrubs, mask, hair cover, and booties come walking out. She felt Cole place his hand on her shoulder and step up behind her for support.

"One of you Mr. Ashton?" the doctor asked as he pulled off the mask.

"I am." Will stepped forward, clearly worried.

"I am Dr. Kejewski. Your wife is awake and asking for you. She was shot through the shoulder. She was lucky. The bullet somehow missed all vital arteries and veins. She was treated for tetanus and is now on some pain meds and IV antibiotics. Some physical therapy and she'll be back to normal in a couple of months." Will audibly exhaled as Mo came up behind him and clasped his shoulder.

"What about Danielle De Luca? She's my fiancé." Mo asked.

"I checked on my way out here. She's still in surgery. It appears she has a punctured lung. The bullet seems to have hit a rib, splintering it into her lung. As they worked to stabilize her, they were able to remove the bullet. They are working on reinflating the lung now. Her doctor will come out and give you a more detailed update when she gets her stabilized." The doctor nodded to the group when no more questions were asked and walked back toward the double doors.

Paige stepped forward and faced Mo. She saw anguish and anxiety in his face. She slipped her arm around Mo and pulled him to her. Will squeezed his shoulder as Cole reached around Paige and offered his support. Paige looked up and saw tears slowly rolling down Mo's stony face. The doctor turned back to the group at the door. Paige's breath caught in her throat. They couldn't take any more bad news.

"Oh, Mr. Ashton, you don't need to worry. The baby is fine."

"Baby?" Will choked out. The group stopped. No one moved. They all stared at Will.

"She's eight weeks along, didn't you know?" The doctor paused and looked at the stunned faces of the group. "Well, obviously not by your reaction. The heartbeat is strong. I don't think you have to worry about a miscarriage. You'll be able to go back to see her shortly. A nurse will come get you once we have her settled into a room." The doctor pushed through the doors and disappeared from sight.

"A baby?" Will's knees buckled and Cole caught him before he fell to the floor. Will got his legs under him enough to be half-led and half-dragged to the nearest chair. "Did I hear that right? Did that doctor say my wife is going to have a baby?" Will asked the group.

"Congratulations. It's wonderful news all around. Kenna is going to fully recover and you're going to be a father," Cole said as he thumped Will on the back. He turned to Mo then. "It's a good sign, Mo. Everything will be alright with Dani. I just know it."

Chapter Three

The group sat in the lobby and stared at the floor. Paige tapped her fingers on the arms of the chair, Will's knee bounced, and Mo sat completely still, interlocking his fingers hard enough to turn the knuckles white. The ER nurse in the teddy bear scrubs pushed through the double doors, gaining everyone's immediate attention.

"Mr. Ashton?"

"That's me." Will stood up on his still shaky legs and stepped forward.

"Ready to go see your wife?"

"More than you'll ever know." Will followed the nurse through the doors after giving Mo a quick hug and smiling to the rest of the group. "I'll tell her y'all are thinking about her."

After that, the doors to the emergency room should have just been left open. Dani's parents, the Rose sisters, and even Mo's parents arrived. The whole town of Keeneston was finding a reason to stop by the emergency room. Seats filled, prayers were said, and baskets were dropped off with cupcakes, brownies, and cookies. Soft blankets and flowers were delivered from members of the community for the next several hours.

Paige spent the time alternating between pacing the room and running interference on the curious crowd who all wanted to talk to Mo. Paige finally sat down in the uncomfortable blue plastic chair and held onto Mo's shaky hand. Every time the doors swooshed open, he would jump to see if they had information on Danielle. Finally a doctor came through the lobby and walked to the waiting area. Paige felt Mo tense and heard the Rose sisters begin to pray.

"Mr. Ali Rahman?" The short woman wearing green scrubs, with curly brown hair haphazardly pulled back into a ponytail, asked the group. Mo stood and stepped forward as if he was facing an executioner.

Paige found herself on her feet. She was so nervous she was shaking. Cole's warm supportive arm slipped around her waist and she was pulled against his strong chest. She took a deep breath to steady herself and found Cole's masculine scent a comfort. He exuded quiet confidence and support as he gently squeezed her hip to show her he was thinking of her.

"How is she?" Mo asked so quietly Paige could barely hear him.

"Stable." Paige saw Mo practically collapse. His father came up beside him, placing his arm around his son's shoulder. Paige couldn't relax yet. She had to hear it all before she could breathe a sigh of relief. She looked to the left of Mo and saw Mr. De Luca with his arm around his wife, tears streaming down his face.

"I'm Dr. Francis, Danielle's surgeon. The bullet hit the rib, shattering it. The rib punctured the left lung, causing it to collapse and resulting in a hemothorax. That's when blood fills the space between the lining of the lung and the collapsed lung. It is what caused Danielle to have such difficulty breathing and what resulted in her losing consciousness.

"We inserted a chest tube into the lung cavity and connected it to a vacuum to drain the fluid and reinflate the lung. At the same time, we removed the bullet. She pulled through very well. She's awake and resting as comfortably as we can make her in the ICU."

"What happens now?" Mo asked.

"The chest tube will stay in until it is no longer draining blood. I would expect at least three or four days. Barring infection or any complications, she could be released in one to two weeks, depending on how she responds to treatment."

"Can I see her now?"

"Yes. She's groggy from the medication, but it will do her good to see her family." Dr. Francis looked around to the large group and frowned. "I can't let you all back there. She needs her rest. Only immediate family, sorry."

"I am Tony De Luca. I am her father, and this is her mother. Could the three of us go back now?" He asked as Mary De Luca embraced a visibly affected Mo in a tight hug.

"Yes, that should be fine. Follow me." With Mary's arm around him, Mo followed Dr. Francis through the door.

Paige finally allowed herself to close her eyes and give thanks. She swayed and leaned against Cole. It was as if all strength and energy had drained from her. She was so tired, so weak. She felt him move his hand up to her shoulder and pull her against him. She let her head fall against his chest and listened to his strong heartbeat. Cole leaned down and rested his cheek against her head.

"It'll be okay. I promise. I need to interview them now. I don't want to leave you here, though. I need to make sure you are safe. I won't be able to focus on my job knowing you are in danger." She felt him gently kiss her head as he talked.

"I'm fine, Cole." Paige nuzzled her head into his chest and took a deep breath. If she could, she'd fall asleep curled into Cole. Huh? No, she wouldn't. She was delirious after a day filled with terror. That must be it.

"No, you're not. You're just too stubborn to realize it," he whispered into her hair.

"I am not! Why you..." She pulled her head back and looked into his eyes. The silver sharpening as his temper rose.

"Paige. Stop. I get it. You don't want to go into protective custody. But I can't work if I am constantly worried about you. So why don't you just come with me? I will know you are safe if I can keep an eye on you." He moved his hand to her head and pulled her close again. She let her head fall back onto his shoulder and thought maybe Cole wasn't as bad as he seemed.

"You mean I can come see Dani and Kenna with you?" She was so relieved she almost kissed Cole right there in the waiting room. Wait. Kiss Cole? Oh no. That would not be a good idea. They would likely run screaming from each other or spontaneously combust. Either way, it was too much for her to think about right now.

"Yes. You'd get to see them. But before you jump in and take over like you are prone to do, I need to ask them questions to get their take on what happened before you fill in any pieces for them. I don't want you accidentally confusing their testimony."

"Deal! Thank you, Cole." She rose up on her toes and placed a quick kiss on his cheek before she could even think about it.

Paige followed Cole over to the nurses' station.

"I need to see McKenna Ashton and Danielle De Luca. Can you give me their room numbers and buzz us back, please."

"Sorry, immediate family only," the young nurse in cupcake-dotted scrubs said as she filled out a chart, never looking up to where Cole had opened his badge.

"Immediate family and FBI only sounds like a good policy." He tapped his badge on the desk and waited for the nurse to look up and examine it.

"Okay. Ashton is in ER room 23. She'll be moved up to a regular room in the next few hours. I think we'll have her in 429. De Luca is in the ICU, bed six."

"Thank you. While you are looking that up, is there any way to put down that I want their records completely private. You can't even acknowledge they are here or if you ever heard of them if anyone who calls."

"Sure. I can do that." The nurse started typing away. "They need extra security?"

"Yes. Danielle De Luca is the fiancée of the Sheik of Rahmi. He'll be providing private security as well. Please make sure you accommodate them. Further, McKenna Ashton is the wife of Will Ashton."

"You mean UK quarterback Will Ashton who threw for 4,358 yards his senior season?"

Cole had managed to grab the nurse's attention with that. Diplomat, siplomat... but a UK football legend was something else entirely.

"One and the same. Also, when it comes time for Danielle to be moved, can you try to put her close to Kenna? It will be easier on the guards and the nurses, for that matter."

"No prob. Hold on, I am just notifying security and the nurses on the fourth floor. Can I classify De Luca as a diplomat? That would allow a lot more leeway for the security team. I can also classify Ashton as a celebrity for further safety measures."

"Yes, that's fine." Cole reached back into his wallet and pulled out a business card and handed it to the nurse. "Here's my contact information. I want to know the second someone calls inquiring about either woman. I also want to know if anyone stops by. If anyone does who is not cleared by me, make sure security saves the footage for me to review."

"Got it. I'll spread the word in the nurses' station. We'll keep a good eye on them."

"Thank you." Cole slipped his hand into hers as he heard the ER doors buzz open. They walked past the nurses' station and the ER chart board. A nurse was already there erasing Kenna and Dani's names and replacing them with Jane Doe 1 and 2.

They walked down a long corridor until they reached another station. They were instantly pointed in the right direction and found Room 23. Paige stood on her tiptoes and tried to look over his shoulder into Kenna's room. It wasn't an easy task considering he was just over six feet tall, a good six inches taller than her. She smiled as she saw Will sitting next to the bed holding Kenna's hand. They were smiling.

"Paige! We're going to have a baby!" Kenna squealed over Cole. Forgetting her promise to let Cole do all the talking first, Paige pushed past him and rushed to Will's side of the bed to give her a gentle hug. As quickly as the celebrations occurred, the mood turned somber.

"How's Dani? Please tell me she's okay." Kenna gripped her hand tightly.

"She's stable. The bullet cracked a rib causing it to puncture and collapse her lung. They are draining the blood now and reinflating the lung," Cole explained. "I am sorry to have to ask you, but can you tell me what you remember about the shooting?" Cole pulled out his ever-present digital recorder and pushed Record.

"Not much. Dani and I were talking about her engagement. We walked through the door and out into the parking lot. I remember putting my arm around her and then I heard the gunshots. Before I could react, I felt the bullet go through my arm. The force knocked me back and I knocked myself out when my head hit the pavement."

"Did you see where the shots were fired from?"

"No. I didn't see anything. I couldn't even tell where the noise was coming from. I am sorry, Cole." Will moved to sit on the bed and pulled his wife close to him.

"There is nothing to apologize for." Cole paused and ran his hand over his head in an action now familiar to Paige. "I guess we know what Plan B is now."

"Yes, but we don't know who carried it out. Obviously it wasn't Edwards or Chad," Kenna said as she leaned her head against Will's chest.

"That's where you are wrong. Paige saw the shooter and is the only one who can identify him. If he is any kind of professional, then he'll be back for her soon."

"But how would he know to come back for her?" Kenna asked.

"Um, I kinda chased him down and we came eye-to-eye before he tried to run me over with his car."

"Oh, Paige!"

"I'll be fine, Kenna. Please don't worry. Just take care of yourself and that baby." She smiled when Kenna instantly moved her hand to cover her abdomen.

"I have tried to get her to go into protective custody, but she refuses," Cole complained.

"I can't go into protective custody. I have Chuck waiting for me at home and I am not about to leave him or my store."

"Chuck? Just who the hell is Chuck and why is he at your home?" Cole's silver eyes snapped in anger.

Paige stood up and walked up to Agent Asshole. It didn't matter that for a couple of seconds she was crazy enough to be thankful he was there comforting her. Now his true persona was back: the over-protective jerk.

"It's none of your business."

"It's my business when I am trying to keep you alive."

She stood still and took in a deep breath of air and tried to rein in her temper. She listened to the beeping of the machines and the ever-present white noise of the air-conditioning. She had always been the one with a short fuse in her family. Most of the time her brothers just laughed at her and didn't take her seriously, which was probably why she tended to get offended pretty easily. But Kenna was injured and clearly upset about her being in danger. She didn't want to make it any worse so she took a deep breath and smiled at Cole.

"Chuck is my dog and I am not leaving my store, okay?" She smiled again at him with all the Southern manners she possessed.

"Fine. You can stay at your store provided I am there with you at all times."

"No way!" Manners be damned. They were overrated anyway.

"It's either me or the safe house, sweetheart."

Paige said goodbye to Kenna and Will and left them discussing which room to turn into a nursery.

"Are you seriously going to move in with me?"

"Yup."

"Won't that be kinda obvious to the assassin? Should I hang an 'FBI Agent Here' sign just in case he misses you strutting around with your gun?"

"Don't be a smart-ass. I'll think of a cover. Now knock off the pissy attitude before we get to Danielle. And do not tell her you saw the shooter. I want her focused completely on her recovery and not worried about you." Cole led her through a maze of corridors and finally she saw the sign for the ICU. He pushed the button and waited to identify himself.

"Okay, but only because I agree with you. Why did you tell Kenna?"

"She was strong enough to handle it. Shoulder shots hurt like a bitch, but they aren't fatal." He spoke into the intercom once it was picked up. "Cole Parker of the FBI here to see Danielle De Luca." The doors opened and they walked through into the ICU.

The ICU was very different from the ER. Lights were dimmed as much as possible. No radios or televisions cranked up. Nurses spoke in hushed tones. No doctors shouting out orders. A security guard approached Cole with his hand on his weapon.

"ID please."

"Sure thing." Cole handed him his badge and waited.

"Thank you."

"No problem. You got up here fast. Is anyone going to McKenna Ashton's room?"

"Yes. A guard will be there shortly. He'll lap the ER as to not draw attention but will look into Mrs. Ashton's room every five minutes."

"Great. Thank you." Cole looked around the room and then pointed to the far side. "Come on, sweetheart, she's right over there."

Paige chose to ignore that her heart fluttered when Cole called her sweetheart. She simply wrote it off as a byproduct of anger. But when Cole slipped his hand back into hers and absently started rubbing his thumb over her knuckles, she couldn't think of any reason to write off the somersaults her stomach was doing.

The sliding glass door was partially closed and the curtain behind it was drawn. Cole knocked quietly on the glass door and waited for the curtain to be pushed aside. Mary De Luca's sharp blue eyes peered around and then softened when she saw Cole and Paige.

"I am so glad you are here. Danielle is demanding information on Kenna and we just don't know the answers. We actually thought you would be the security Ahmed is sending over." Mary pulled the curtain back and allowed them to squeeze in. It was going to be a tight fit.

Paige looked around the dim room and saw Mo sitting similarly to Will, right next to the bed and holding onto Dani's hand as if he expected her to run away. Dani's father sat at the foot of the bed, clearly thinking he was going to protect her from anyone who didn't belong. Mary went around the bed and took a seat on Dani's other side and smiled at them. Dani was propped up slightly and looked so pale she could blend in with the hospital sheets. A plastic tube extended from her left side and connected to a machine. It looked like Mary had tried her best to wash the blood off and braid her long dark brown hair.

"Paige! How is Kenna? Mo told me she was stable, but we haven't gotten any new updates since then." Cole turned his body sideways so she could slide past him. She turned her body sideways and squeezed all the way into the room. She was very aware of every inch of Cole's body pressed against her back.

"She's doing great. We just came from seeing her. Her shoulder wound will heal in a couple of months with the help of physical therapy. Did Mo tell you the big news?"

"Big news?" Dani's brow knit slightly as she thought about it. "No, I don't think so."

"Kenna and Will are going to have a baby!"

"No way!"

"Yup. She's eight weeks along and the baby has a strong heartbeat and is doing fine." Dani grinned at the group and then turned and gave The Look to Mo.

"And why didn't you tell me?"

"I sorta forgot. I was so worried about you that it went right out of my mind. I am sorry, honey."

"I can't stay mad at you for that. But I want more updates even if you have to bribe the nurses." Dani yawned and Paige saw her eyes start to drift shut. Cole cleared his throat and her eyes snapped back open.

"I am sorry, Danielle, but I have some questions for you. Then we'll leave you to get some rest. Do you mind?" Cole gently asked.

"Of course not. Do you know who did this?"

"Not yet. But we're looking into a lead." Cole pulled out his digital recorder and slid his arm around Paige's waist to get a clear recording. "Can you tell me what happened?"

"Sure. Kenna had just finished a case with the chronic masturbator and we hurried out of court to meet Paige at the cafe. I pushed open the side door. Kenna and I were talking about the engagement and she put her arm around my shoulder as we were laughing. Then I heard the two shots. I looked to Kenna, getting ready to ask her if she knew where they came from, but she was lying on the ground, already unconscious. I tried to say her name, but it felt like I was drowning. I couldn't get a breath. It was only then that I looked down at myself and saw the blood and I realized I was shot. I am sorry, but I blacked out then."

"Could you tell where the shot was coming from?" Cole asked.

"I have a good guess thanks to growing up around guns," she smiled at her mother. "I would say from across the street on one of the roofs. On top of the cafe would be the most likely place."

"Why would you say that?"

"It's a clear shot to both the front door and only a slight adjustment for people exiting from the side. The angle would be too much for a clear shot on those exiting the side from farther down Main Street and the angle too great for the front door if farther up Main Street. I take it I am right?"

"You're right. The shooter was on top the cafe. You didn't happen to see anything, did you?"

"No. Just heard it and immediately turned to ask Kenna. I should have followed the shot. Maybe I could have seen the shooter then before I passed out."

"Do not worry, Danielle. We have a description we are working on. Too many people around for no one to see anything. You did a great job. I am very impressed you were able to diagnose the location of the shot. Paige, how about we let Dani rest?" Cole rested his hand on her hip and pulled her even closer against him.

"Okay. Dani, do you need anything? What did your doctor say?"

"Thanks, Paige. No, I don't need anything right now. Dr. Francis said everything went well. I just have to have this tube in for a couple of days. Then respiratory therapy. She is hopeful that I will have a full recovery."

"Good. We'll let you rest then. Call me if you need anything." Dani gave a weak smile and a slight nod before her eyes drifted shut again.

Cole angled out of the room and, after waving to the group, Paige followed him out of the ICU and into the maze of corridors.

"I think all my adrenalin has worn off. I am about to crash, too." Although, if Cole kept finding reasons to touch her, she was pretty sure sleep was going to be the last thing on her mind.

"Not so fast. You still have to meet with a sketch artist. Red is rounding one up now." Cole laced his fingers through hers and gave her a gentle tug. He looked down at her and smiled. Oh my. Cole smiling was not something she was used to seeing. The cold steel of his silver eyes melted and he went from cold, hard lawman to sexy lawman in a split second. "Come on, take me home."

Chapter Four

Cole placed his hand on the small of her back and guided her through the emergency room lobby. As the day grew into night, the lobby became more crowded. She looked through the glass doors and into the dark night and moved closer to Cole. She had held up well since lunch. But now that the panic and worry were over, the fear was wrapping its cold hands around her heart.

"Paige, wait." Cole slid his hand from her back and grasped her arm to stop her. "We don't know if the assassin is out there. To best protect Kenna and Dani, we need to give off the impression that he was successful. Just in case he's watching, let's give him a show." He slid his arm around her shoulder and pulled her head against his chest.

"This is stupid, Cole."

"No, it's not. He's going to need confirmation of the deaths. If we walk out of here as if everything is going to be fine, then there is a greater chance he'll try to complete his job."

"Oh well, if you put it that way it doesn't sounds so stupid." She buried her face in his shirt and leaned against him as they made their way out to the parking lot. She closed her eyes and stumbled.

"Good, keep it up. My car is just a few more yards away," Cole whispered into her hair. The sad thing was that the stumble was real. Now that she was leaning on someone else and had made the mistake of closing her eyes, she felt the exhaustion of the day setting in. All she wanted was to crawl into bed and sleep. Cole would be great to sleep with the way his body was radiating heat. She bet her feet wouldn't even get cold. In fact, she bet she'd be warm all over.

"Shit, sorry." Paige stumbled over Cole's foot and fell into him, clinging to prevent herself from falling face first onto the pavement. Embarrassed about the way her thoughts were turning, she pushed back from him, tripped over his foot again, and slammed against the passenger door of a black Ford Explorer.

"Glad you found the car. You alright?" Cole gave her a little smirk that made her face flame. She didn't know how, but she knew that he knew the directions of her thoughts.

"Um, yeah. Fine." Smooth Paige. She stepped back from the door and Cole opened it for her. She slid into the standard government vehicle and closed her eyes while Cole walked around. This was no good. There was no way she'd keep her sanity if he moved in with her. She heard him open his door and slide into his seat.

"So, I was thinking. I don't think it's a good idea if you stay at my place. I don't have a lot of room and I certainly don't have time. I am getting ready for the back-to-school sales and the Summer Festival. I just don't have time to think of an explanation as to why there is an FBI agent following me around. You'd just get in my way and slow me down." Paige couldn't seem to meet his eye. She kept her vision firmly fixed on the yellow lines of the road in front of them.

"No." Cole's tone was cold and even. It sounded almost like a threat. Embarrassment be damned, she wasn't going to let him tell her what to do. She whipped her head around and stared at his profile. His silver eyes reflected the low green lights of the driver's controls and his slightly crooked nose gave his looks a more dangerous slant.

"No, what?" Paige snapped. Cole slowly turned his head and looked at her.

"No, I am not letting you out of my sight. No, I am not letting you talk your way out of protection. No, I don't want to hear all your ideas on the matter. Your safety and how to go about it is my job, my responsibility. I have things under control, Paige. You just need to trust me."

Paige snorted. Trust him, yeah right.

Cole turned back to the road and turned toward Keeneston. "I can't believe you just snorted. I'll have you know I am quite trustworthy." Paige saw his lips curl up into a smirk and fought the urge to smack him on the head.

"Where are you taking me?" Paige asked as they passed the "Welcome to Keeneston" sign.

"I am taking you home. Where else would I take you?"

"How do you know where I live?" Paige would remember if she told him she lived above her shop. It wasn't a secret or anything, but she didn't have a landline and her address was a post office box.

"I am in the FBI. We are kinda good at finding things." This time the bastard didn't even try to hide the grin.

It was dark out, but downtown was awash in the soft glow of the old-fashioned street lamps. With the summer days being so hot, most people went out for their daily strolls at night. Paige saw the people on the sidewalk stop and stare when they stopped at the first stoplight in Keeneston.

"Oh no. I forgot it gets so crowded at night." Paige closed her eyes and her ears started twitching at the hum coming from the chatter moving its way up the street.

"So?"

"Just watch. Before we get to the next light, the whole town will know we are back and will want to know what's going on. See there." Paige pointed to the heavy man in suspenders standing near the car on the sidewalk. "That's John Wolfe, and see that elderly woman with the walker practically running up the sidewalk toward the cafe? Well, that's one of Miss Lily's neighbors, Edna Schniter."

"She's going to break a hip if she's not careful."

"Well, she's going to tell that family there, the Gilberts. Pam is the president of the PTA and all-around perfect soccer mom. She's going to send one of her kids up to the cafe to alert everyone there that we are back in town. Then, by the time we get to the next stoplight, the whole cafe will be outside waiting for us."

"Yeah right. Why would Edna or John or the Gilberts care? And these windows are tinted, they can't even tell who is in here." Cole shook his head and Paige just smiled.

"I'll bet fifty bucks I am right," she held her hand out to shake on it.

"Deal. Easy money, Davies, easy money." He placed his hand in hers and shook it. She looked up at him and their eyes locked. She broke the eye contact and looked down to where he was still holding her hand. Oh, this was not good. If this kept going, she might have to acknowledge Cole was different from the others and she wasn't ready to do that yet.

"Light's green."

Cole slowly pulled his hand away and placed it on the steering wheel.

"I'll be damned. I owe you fifty bucks, Davies." Paige followed where Cole was looking and saw Miss Daisy, Miss Violet, and about twenty other people gathering on the sidewalk outside the cafe waiting for them to drive by. Miss Violet was standing there waving a towel in the air to get their attention, as if the mob didn't do that already.

"You better let me handle this. You'll be all governmental and then Miss Daisy will smack you with that serving spoon she's holding."

"Don't say anything. We need them to believe Kenna and Dani are dead so the shooter will think so, too."

Paige rolled her eyes but didn't say anything. That would never fly in town. The Rose sisters were notorious for telling when someone was lying. The CIA and FBI had nothing on them. Further, John Wolfe would somehow ferret out the truth and then it would spread, unchecked. She pushed the auto window button as she waited for Cole to stop his car at the next stoplight. As soon as the car stopped, the Rose sisters were at the window.

"How are our girls?" Miss Daisy asked as she reached inside and grabbed her hand, squeezing it tight to express her worry.

"Anyone new been in town today?" Paige asked them.

"Not at the cafe, let me check with some of the others." Miss Daisy turned away and started working her way through the crowd.

"So, they're still in danger. At least that means they are alive." Miss Violet said a quick prayer for their safety.

"We're sorry to inform you, neither McKenna nor Dani survived the shooting," Cole interrupted. Paige closed her eyes and said her own prayer. Agent Asshole at work again. If she didn't think he deserved it, she'd feel bad for what was about to happen.

"Young man, I know you are a federal agent, and I know you have helped our girls out, but don't you ever lie to me again, do you understand me? Hasn't anyone ever told you? You are not a good liar, bless your heart. Now cut the bologna and tell me what's really going on." Miss Violet leveled her stare at Cole.

"I told you, they didn't make…"

"Cole Parker, don't even try it. This is your last warning before I cut you off from the cafe. Now, why don't you just sit there and look handsome while the women talk." Miss Violet ignored the outraged look Cole shot them and turned to Paige. "Dear, tell us what has happened."

"Here comes your sister, let's see what she has to say first."

"All clear. No one new snooping around. Just the regular tourists," Miss Daisy reported.

"How do you know they are tourists and not the shooter?" She could tell Cole thought he had them.

"Why don't you just sit there and look pretty. We know what we're doing."

Paige snorted. The look on Cole's face was too much. She had tried to suppress the laugh and snorted instead.

"First, Kenna is fine. A couple months of rehab for the shot to the shoulder and she'll be back to normal. Dani suffered a collapsed lung and is in the ICU. The bullet luckily hit a rib and shattered it but got imbedded in the rib and only partly in the lung. There was surgery to remove the bullet and to clean up the rib the best they could. She'll be in the hospital at least a week. They are cautiously optimistic about a full recovery."

"Oh, love their hearts. We'll all start praying for them. I'll go start the phone tree." Miss Violet started back into the cafe to get the tree going.

"No!" Cole shouted.

"Why ever not, dear?"

"We need the assassin to think they are dead. They'll be safer that way. If he knows they are alive, then he'll have to finish the job." Paige was relieved when she heard the murmurs of the crowd agreeing with her.

"I can take care of that." A petite woman with mousy-brown hair tied in a loose bun raised her head.

"Marianne! I am so glad you're here tonight. You think you can write up something nice?"

"Sure. I'll put it online right now and then it will go out in the paper day after tomorrow."

"Who's that and what is she going to do?" Cole whispered to Paige.

"She's the owner and operator of the *Keeneston Journal*. She'll put in a nice story about how they died. She's very good. Everyone reads the obits because of how well she treats each one. Lots of papers just stick them in the back, but she puts them in the first section of the paper."

"Thank you, Marianne. That would be a great help to my investigation. Also, can I ask you all to do me a favor?" Cole leaned toward the open window to get everyone's attention. "It is crucial that no one knows they are alive. However, we also have the problem that Paige here saw the shooter and he saw her. He'll be back to finish the job. I need you all to be on the lookout for a man in his forties, no visible tattoos, short brown hair, athletic, and around five-ten. Call me immediately if you see anyone fitting that description. I don't know when, but I would bet my life he'll be around here again real soon trying to find out if the girls are dead and to tie up his one loose end, Paige."

The crowd gasped and Paige was torn between rolling her eyes at his dramatic speech and running to hide under her bed in fear. She knew she was in a serious spot, and she was prepared to face it in the tough girl persona that being raised with five brothers gave you. But, on some level, she knew this was different from walking the roof beam in the hay barn to prove she was just as good as the boys. This was her life. Cole must have noticed the shift in her because he placed his hand on her knee and gave it an encouraging squeeze. She looked down at his hand and groaned again. She hadn't shaved yet this week and her legs were all prickly.

"It'll be okay. Come on, let's get you home." She and Cole waved bye to the group whom the Rose sisters were already herding back into the cafe to formulate some kind of plan.

The second they got close enough to her store to see the cars lining the street, Paige knew she was in trouble. She recognized the sheriff's cruiser and four of her brothers' cars. But, what worried her more was the old white Volvo station wagon belonging to her mother parked right in front of the building.

"Looks like we have a full house tonight." Cole said as he searched for a place to park.

"There's private parking around back. Just turn into that alley there." Paige pointed to the tiny alley between her store and the Keeneston Historical Society. Just moments ago, all she had wanted was to get home and climb into bed. Now, she was thinking the assassin might be the better option. Nothing, absolutely nothing, could terrify her more than her mother. People often thought it was the loud and rowdy Davies men that ruled the house. But it was actually her mother, Marcy Davies, all five-feet seven inches of strawberry blonde hair and bright blue eyes. She was quiet, polite, and ruthless. She could screw you with a smile and you'd thank her, never realizing she had cut you down. She had once asked her mother how she could be so nice and tough at the same time. Her mother had told her to always be a lady, but when you raise five boys you learn to be tough, too.

Cole pulled into the alley and parked next to her cheery, light-yellow building. She was so proud of it. She had bought the building on the courthouse steps for next to nothing and spent months installing new windows, drywall, fixtures, and restoring the hundred-year-old original hardwood floors. She had sewn her own curtains made from a similarly colored yellow, cornflower blue, and white striped fabric trimmed in lace. She had built display tables and made matching tablecloths. She had turned an abandoned historic house into a rejuvenated shop and home. Her heart warmed every time she pushed open her navy-blue door and walked into her shop. However, this time when she pushed open the door, instead of being met with the warm ambient light from her display cases, she was met with all of her lights on, most of her family sitting on the stairs, and a group of sheriff's deputies sitting behind the sales counter.

Before she could open her mouth, her family was up and talking at the same time. Her father, Jake Davies, and her brothers, Miles, Marshall, Cade, and Pierce, all swarmed her with questions about what happened. Only her mother didn't stand up and say a word.

"Where's Cy?" Paige managed to ask before her brothers and father launched into some sort of side conversation or lecture. She didn't know what direction they were heading and thought to cut them off.

"We found him in Switzerland. He said he can be here in a couple of days if we need him," her father answered.

"What is he doing in Switzerland?"

"Who knows, but what were you doing chasing after an armed man?" Miles had his big brother lecture voice on.

"Before you start lecturing your sister, why don't we have her introduce us to this nice young man she's here with?" That was so typical of her mother. She made an FBI escort home sound like a high school date.

"Ma, this is FBI Agent Cole Parker. Cole, this is my mother, Marcy Davies." She and her mother stood at the same height, but that was where their similarities stopped. Her mother's strawberry blonde hair was turning blonder with age. Only Cy had their mother's strawberry blonde hair. Cade was dark-blonde, but all of the other siblings had their father's brown hair. Paige also inherited her father's hazel eyes, as did all her brothers.

Paige watched her mother smile and shake hands with Cole. "It's nice to meet you, ma'am."

"It's nice to meet you, too. This is my husband, Jake Davies." Cole shook his hand and they did the quick once-over measuring each other up. This was her favorite part. Her brothers never behaved themselves when introduced to a man in Paige's life, regardless of their relationship status. "And these are four of my five sons. I think you know the oldest, Miles, and then Marshall."

Miles nodded from where he stood in front of Paige with his hands on his hips. Marshall uncoiled himself from where he was sitting on the stairs and held out his hand for Cole to shake.

"Good to see you both again," Cole said as he shook Marshall's hand. Paige saw him grimace and she smiled. Her brother was an intimidator. He separated the weak members of the suitor herd real fast with one of his bone-crushing handshakes. Paige wouldn't have believed what happened next it if she hadn't seen it. Cole just smiled and adjusted his grip slightly and wiggled his fingers a bit. Marshall gave an involuntary grimace of his own and then the two smiled and thumped each other on the back.

"And this is Cade and my youngest, Pierce." Her mother finished the introductions and moved to stand next to her father. Uh-oh, the united front. She felt them closing in. Sure enough, her parents were off to her left, her brother Miles was in front of her, Marshall was flanking now that the introductions were done. Cade and Pierce moved to her right to block them in. It was solid military procedure to prevent escape.

"Cade, it's good to see you again. Pierce, nice to meet you. I hear you are at UK getting your master's. Good luck with that." Cole shook each their hands and only became aware of their situation when he looked back at Paige. She could tell by the quick look of confusion on his face that he realized they were surrounded by a six-foot wall.

"So, Cole, our sister is in danger. What are you planning to do about it?" Miles kept his voice low, but his tone was hard as steel.

"I plan on staying by her side 24/7 and protecting her from getting herself shot. That's what I plan to do."

Even though she was not too fond of the plan, she had to give Cole props for not shrinking away like so many men before him had done when faced with the full force of the Davies family.

"That's a plan for her immediate safety, but what about her permanent safety?" Marshall asked from behind him.

"That's why those men are here." Cole gestured to Red, Dinky, Noodle, and some middle-aged man with thick black glasses, cargo shorts, and a white polo shirt. Damn. She really didn't want to be impressed, but she was. The whole time Cole talked, he stood still and kept eye contact with Miles, not turning around and around like her brothers wanted him to. "She's going to give a description to the sketch artist and then I will take a copy of the sketch and run it through the FBI database. Red will run it through the Kentucky State Police database. Both runs will produce a flag, meaning it will be sent to every FBI agent in the area and every police officer in the state. The sooner you stop this little mock interrogation, the sooner I can get that sketch out to people who can find this guy."

Paige felt her mouth drop open. No one had ever spoken to Miles like that before. Miles exuded fire and ice with every breath. He could freeze you out with a stare or blister you with words. Paige looked around the circle and found all the men had tensed their jaws at the obvious power play. However, her mother stood with a large smile on her face. She clapped her hands and the spell was broken.

"Come on, Jake. Let's get home. Paige and Cole have work to do. I think we can all say she is in safe hands now." She stepped over to Paige and placed a motherly kiss on her cheek. "See you soon, sweetie."

"Bye, Ma. Bye, Dad."

"Bye-bye, sugar. You give us a call if you need anything, you hear?"

Paige nodded and watched her parents head for their car. "Aren't you all leaving?" she asked her brothers who had pulled in rank again and stood shoulder to shoulder in front of the staircase.

"Not yet," Miles responded. That was it and that was all she was going to get out of him right now.

Forty-five minutes later, Paige sat next to the sketch artist and stared at the man who had shot her best friends. Last time she had seen him, she didn't know what had happened. Now, when she looked at him, she could see the cold depths of his eyes and the hard lines around his mouth.

"Thanks, Pete," Cole shook the sketch artist's hand. "You have a scanner, Paige?"

"Yes. In the back room, there is a computer with a copier and scanner hooked up to it. Just go past the hat room and you'll see the door on your left just under the staircase." Paige watched as Red and Cole went in search of the room. She took a deep breath and slowly let it out. She didn't think anything about doing the sketch but having to focus on that time and stare at the man now trying to kill her had gotten her shook up.

"You okay, Paige?" Pierce had walked around the counter and now stood in front of her.

"It was harder than I thought it would be." Pierce may have been younger by three years, but they felt things as if they were twins. Pierce was a nerdy kid growing up, tall and skinny with sharp elbows and knees. He was captain of the math team, played the trumpet in band, and was the president of the Future Farmers of America. Paige had always theorized that because he wasn't chased after like her other brothers, Pierce could sit back and watch. He could read emotions and body language even better than her mother. Even after he grew into his body and became the most handsome of all the brothers, he still tried to stay out of the limelight. He was quiet, confident, and always stood up for others who either couldn't or were too afraid to do it themselves.

"Okay. We got it sent out to all law enforcement. I have also printed off enough copies to take to the businesses around town so they can help keep a look out for you, too," Cole said as he walked out of the back room with Red.

"You look tired, Sis. How about you go on upstairs and climb into bed." Pierce gave her a quick peck on the forehead and helped her up from her chair. Now that he mentioned it, she was tired. Her legs felt as if they were in quicksand, and her whole body pulsed with weariness.

"Sounds like a plan I can agree with. She walked past Pierce and got a kiss on the head from each brother as she passed them. She was halfway up the stairs when she remembered Cole. She turned around and found him surrounded by her brothers—again.

"Don't worry, Sis. He'll be up in a minute. We just need to have a quick chat with him."

"Miles, you do realize I am not seventeen anymore, right? And you do realize that Cole isn't my boyfriend, right?" She was too tired for this.

She turned back around and had almost made it to the landing when she heard Marshall mumble, "You may think he's not your boyfriend, but I think he thinks differently."

Paige somehow managed to make it up the stairs and unlock the door leading into her living area. The first room she entered was a large living room. She had painstakingly made it hers, buying furniture piece by piece until she had the whole set. The result was a large espresso-colored couch that sat in front of the fireplace with a matching loveseat and chair finishing off the room. A slate table sat in front of the couch and a flat-screen television hung over the fireplace. Bookshelves lined the wall on both sides of the fireplace and were full of pictures of her family, books, and magazines. If she walked straight through the room, she would go into the kitchen with the outdated appliances and oak cabinets. She had a small kitchen table that sat two and an island she used to try out some of her crafts. There was an old door that led out to a metal fire escape/back stairway. It was technically a walk-up, but was made from the same durable but ugly metal as fire escapes. She used it to take Chuck out at night since there was a small city park behind her house.

Instead of going to the kitchen, Paige turned left through the archway and went past her half-bath before turning right down the main hallway. Back here, she had two bedrooms and a full bath between them. She had turned the smaller bedroom into her office and the large bedroom into the master. She had personally selected the chocolate and ivory theme. She had ivory walls with colorful pictures and paintings on the wall. The carpet was thick and chocolate-colored. Her bedspread was ivory, while her sheets were chocolate. She had found all her furniture at the local antique stores and spent a month sanding them down and finishing with a coat of varnish to let the natural glow of the wood come through.

As normal, her best friend was lying on top of her bed pillows. She had found Chuck on her parents' farm one night. He was trying to crawl through the fence but was too weak to make it all the way through. She had gone for a walk and saw him slumped over the bottom plank. At first she had thought he was dead. But when he opened his chocolate-brown eyes and pleaded with her, she turned into Superwoman. She ripped the board down and scooped him up. He was part chocolate lab and part Lord only knows. His ears were bleeding and his back end wasn't working. She ran home with him in her arms.

Her father had called Dr. Truett and he had rushed over to try to save him. Dr. Truett pulled buckshot from his ears and had to saw off the rope collar imbedded on his neck. He had either been hit by a car or beaten so much that his hip socket was shattered, causing his long tail to be off center. He had made it through the night and by the next morning was wolfing down bowls of dog food. She moved him home with her to continue to nurse him back to health and a month later had a seventy-five-pound mixed-breed that refused to leave her side.

As she sat down on the bed next to Chuck, he thumped his tail against the pillow to say, "Welcome home." She untied her shoelaces and kicked them off when she heard the bell over the front door sound. Either Cy had flown in from Switzerland and was joining the band of brothers to try to intimidate Cole, or they had finally given up and headed home. Her question was answered when she heard the footsteps coming down the hall.

"Hey. So, that was fun. They do that to everyone you know?" Cole strode into her bedroom as if he belonged there. "Whoa. That is one ugly dog."

At the noise of someone coming into the house that he didn't know, Chuck had jumped up from his nest and placed himself at the end of the bed, squarely between the intruder and Paige. His hair raised and he let out a low growl as Cole walked farther into the room.

"He's not ugly!" Paige defended. She put her arm around the tree trunk of a neck and pulled him over to her as if to shield him from the mean words.

"What's with the ears? They stick straight out the side of his head. They don't perk up and they don't fall forward, they just stick straight out." Cole cocked his head and stared at Chuck for a second. He snapped his fingers. "I got it. My mom used to watch reruns of the 'Flying Nun' with Sally Fields when she was ironing. That's what his ears look like!"

Paige picked up the pillow Chuck's butt had just been resting on and threw it at Cole, hitting him right in the face as he laughed. "Here. You can sleep on the couch. And for making fun of my dog, you don't get a blanket."

"I am not making fun of him. Is there something wrong with his tail?" He laughed.

"Chuck, attack," Paige said calmly as she folded her arms underneath her breasts. Chuck jumped down from the bed and started to slowly stalk Cole.

"Okay, okay. I am sorry if I offended you, Chuck. I gotta like any dog that protects his owner like you do." Cole squatted to the ground and waited for Chuck to reach him. Chuck then attacked with a flurry of wet dog kisses, knocking Cole to the floor.

"Come on, big boy, how about I take you for a walk while your mommy finds me a blanket?" Cole scratched behind Chuck's ear as he stood up. Her dog walked out of the room with Cole and never glanced back.

Chapter Five

C ole's silver eyes shone as he looked down at her. He traced
the outline of her cheek and jaw with his fingertip before
lowering his lips to hers. It was a kiss of dreams. So powerful
she felt like she was spinning out of control. His hands moved over
her as he rolled her on top of him.

Thump! "Aw, shit." Paige landed on the floor on her stomach,
cushioned by her pillow version of Cole. She tossed the pillow she
was holding back onto the bed as she rubbed her hip. She'd never
fallen out of bed before and was just plain embarrassed.

Chuck leaned his head over the side of the bed and stared down
at her with his ears sticking straight out. "You better not say
anything, traitor. You just went off with him like he was your best
friend." Chuck just wagged his tail.

Paige sniffed the air and could have sworn she smelled coffee.
That couldn't be. She didn't even know where her coffee pot was.
She had tried making it a couple of times, but it had turned out so
awful she gave up and just got coffee at the cafe before work every
day. She quickly pulled out a pair of khaki shorts and a white tank
top before heading for the kitchen with Chuck galloping ahead of
her.

"Hey there, big boy." Cole scratched Chuck's ear as his clumsy
tail beat against the table leg. Cole slid a muffin out of a basket sitting
on her island and fed it to him, wrapper and all. Paige took a

moment to enjoy the view of his backside as he continued to scratch Chuck's ear. "Where's your mommy? Do you need to go out?"

Paige felt her face flush as she thought about those hands working their magic on her in her dream. And, of course, he just had to turn around and look at her then. He gave her a little wink and she just knew he somehow knew she'd been staring at his ass and that she'd had one heck of a dream about him.

"Morning, sunshine. Miss Daisy dropped off some breakfast for us. She said it was proper mourning food and warned us the rest of the town will be by throughout the day to keep up appearances." Cole held out the basket and she selected a chocolate walnut muffin.

"So what exactly is your plan here? I still don't understand how you are going to follow me around everywhere and not tip the guy off that you're FBI. Or are you going to follow me around in your FBI baseball cap and windbreaker?" She bit into the muffin and sighed. Maybe on top of the coffee she'd have to beg Miss Violet to make these muffins for her everyday, too.

"No. I am not going to run around looking like Ahmed all scary and in black. I want to blend in and hopefully catch this guy scoping out the area."

"Good luck with that. I think it will be pretty obvious that you're law enforcement if you are around me all the time." Paige took another bite of the muffin and closed her eyes as the chocolate slowly melted over her tongue. Heaven.

"Well, there is one way." Cole refilled his coffee mug and waited for her to open her eyes and look at him. "I am going to be your new employee in the store." Paige laughed and choked on her muffin.

"You expect me to believe that you'd work in a store like mine? My brothers don't even like coming in here. And if we manage to pull off the employee angle, how are we going to explain your presence during non-work hours?"

Cole leaned a hip against the island and smiled. The flush that came instantly to her face couldn't be stopped. He was one sexy man and when he smiled that smile with a hint of smirk, it told the world he knew something they didn't. It was irresistible.

"Actually, I have a solution to both of those problems. It would answer why I would take a job in a powder puff of a store and why we were together after work."

"Well..." Paige tapped her foot and raised her eyebrows. She hated the feeling of being left in the dark. She liked to be in control. And there was the rub between her and Cole. They both liked being in control.

"I'm Cole Parker, your live-in boyfriend who is madly in love with you." Cole uncrossed his leg and pushed himself off the counter. Paige was so shocked she just stood there processing what he said over and over again. Cole took a step forward and wrapped his arms around her waist and lowered his lips to her ear. "It's okay, sweetheart. There're a lot of benefits to having me as a boyfriend," he whispered. Cole stepped back, smiled at her stunned expression and walked out the back door with her dog.

"What the hell just happened?" she asked Chuck before realizing her dog had left her again.

Paige rushed out of the shower and flung open her closet. She was ten minutes late to open the store and with the Summer Festival coming up, she had a lot of work to do. She grabbed a belted navy jersey dress from Old Navy and slipped it over her wet hair. She found some red sandals and slipped them on as she blasted her hair with the dryer. She grabbed one of her new red ribbon bows and twisted her hair into a loose-fitting ponytail.

She applied some lip gloss and went back to her closet to fetch a long red scarf. Taking off the navy belt, she slipped the scarf through the rings and tied it in a knot at her side. There. Even Cole would have to admit she looked pretty good, not that she took longer than normal getting ready for him this morning.

She opened the door at the top of the stairs and bounced down to the landing. She was just excited to get to work. It was definitely not because Cole was downstairs, she told herself. She was about to turn on the landing and head down into her shop when she heard something that was enough to make her blood turn to ice and the hairs on the back of her neck stand at attention. It was a giggle. It was a fake giggle that reminded her of nails on a chalkboard. And that giggle only belonged to one person. Kandi Chase-Rawlings, her lifelong archenemy.

Paige crept down the stairs far enough to be able to lean forward and see where Kandi was standing near the sales counter in full slut mode. Her white tank top was two sizes too small for her plastic double D's that stuck out and pointed at Cole. Her miniskirt barely covered her perfectly toned ass that she showed off to perfection when she "accidentally" dropped her purse and had to turn and pick it up. Her long, bottle-dyed blonde hair was curled in loose waves flowing down her back and expertly flicked over her shoulders.

"I just got back from the summer at the lake. I didn't know Paige had hired help. It's nice to see she at least has taste in that." Kandi ran her manicured fingernail down Cole's muscled arm. Paige jumped back on the stairs and took a deep breath. She knew Cole was her fake boyfriend. She knew she had no claim on him, but this was history repeating itself and she wasn't about to let Kandi ruin her life a second time.

Paige took a deep breath to calm herself. It wouldn't do any good to assault a woman right in front of a federal officer. She plastered on her sweeter-than-sugar smile and tried to stop the anger that was making her shake.

"Kandi! It's so nice to see you again. How was your trip to the lake?" Paige made her grand entrance down the stairs pretending to be Scarlett O'Hara.

"It was divine. Too bad you can't afford to do something like that yourself." Kandi smiled and flashed her overly bleached teeth.

"How are Bill and the kids? Cole, dear, did you know that Kandi here has been married nine years already? And how old are your kids now? Ten and eight?" Paige smiled again and even threw in an innocent bat of her eyelashes.

"That's right, honey. I am fortunate enough to have two wonderful boys. Any man's dream." Paige's smile almost faltered when Kandi pressed her breast against Cole's arm, showing him pictures of her boys in football uniforms.

"That's great. They seem to enjoy football. I played all the way through college."

"Oooh. That's wonderful. Where did you go to college?" Kandi turned to look at Cole and managed to shove her breasts out even farther. Maybe she had an air pump in there, like those tennis shoes from the nineties you could pump up.

"Centre College, down in Danville."

"Sexy and smart. Whatever are you doing stuck in this little store then? You should come talk to my husband. He owns Rawlings Car Dealership. I bet he could get you a nice job."

"Aw, gee Kandi. That's nice of you. But see Cole and I are living together and he's happy here with me." She wanted to kiss him when he walked past Kandi and put his arm around her.

"Sure, we all know how long guys stick around you." Kandi giggled her annoying little giggle and Cole tightened his grip on her shoulder. "I'll see you real soon then." Kandi winked at Cole and bent over to pick up her purse she had somehow dropped again.

"Oh, Kandi, I have a cream to help with that cellulite. Make sure you pick some up next time you come in. I sure hope I get to see you soon. It's always such a pleasure." Paige smiled as Kandi huffed out of the store.

"Ewww, that woman!" Paige shook with such anger after her encounter with Kandi that she couldn't stand still. She had to move. She knew what had to be done. She had to organize.

She rounded the corner of the sales counter and pulled out all the pencils, sales receipts, and gift boxes, dumping them on the floor. Cole came around the counter and took a seat next to the register and watched with one eyebrow raised.

"No-good, snooty, man-stealing slut," Paige mumbled to herself as she sprayed the shelf and ferociously wiped it clean. "Coming into my shop, flirting with my imaginary boyfriend." She restacked the gift boxes and moved to the tissue paper dispensers. She then moved to the displays and dusted, shook out the tablecloths, and redesigned the displays all before her next customer came in.

Paige wrapped the homemade bourbon vanilla candle in tissue paper. She had heard Cole's phone ring a couple minutes ago and saw him head upstairs. She was only listening with half an ear as her customer happily prattled on about her granddaughter in college and how she had been enjoying the trip into Keeneston for some gift shopping before the summer family reunion they were having.

Paige smiled and nodded at the appropriate times but couldn't tear her eyes from the staircase. Was there news? Was everything okay with Kenna and Dani? Did the assassin get caught? It was bothering her that this worry was consuming her life. She loved running her shop, but now she flinched every time the bell rang over the door, thinking it could be the assassin coming to finish her off. She loved talking to her clients about their kids, grandkids, horrible mothers-in-law, or how great or horrible their spouses were. It's one of the reasons she worked so much at the counter instead of giving more hours to Betty Jo. But now she couldn't even focus on her client. All she could focus on was her speculation over Cole's call. Maybe it wasn't even about the case. Maybe it was his mother. Or girlfriend? Oh, God, did he have a girlfriend, or worse, was he married? Did it look like that candle display needed to be moved around? She said goodbye to her client and started reorganizing the candle display.

"Uh-oh. Did Kandi come back while I was upstairs?"

"How could you not tell me you were married?" She slammed down one of her new scents and grabbed her dust rag.

"Married? Paige, what are you talking about?" Cole's hands moved to his hips and his posture read pissed-off instead of guilty. Whoops.

"You're not married?"

"No." The cold stare he was directing at her was giving her frostbite. "Whatever made you think I was married?"

"I'm sorry. I was just thinking that I didn't know anything about you and in my stressed state, I just made an illogical jump to that being your wife on the phone." She knew her face was red and she felt as if she had been caught being bad by a teacher. Cole ran his hand through his hair and let out a frustrated breath.

"It's okay. I guess you are right. We don't actually know anything about each other, which could be a problem if we are to be believed to be in a serious relationship. How about we go out on a lunch date and learn more about each other?"

"Um, no thanks. It's not a real relationship anyway. The only person we need to fool is the assassin and he's not going to be quizzing us. So who was on the phone?"

"Just my boss." Cole grinned and she knew he had info.

"Well?"

"Oh, you want to know about the phone call and what news we have?"

"Duh," Paige widened her eyes and threw in an eye roll for good measure.

"We can discuss it over lunch," Cole winked.

"I said no to lunch. We're not really dating, Cole."

"Yet, you cared if I was married. Interesting. Here's the deal, Paige. You let me take you out on a date tonight and I'll tell you what I found out. No date, no info." Oh! She really wanted to wipe that cocky grin off his face, but she really wanted to know what happened.

"Fine. But I don't have to like it." She was saved by the bell, quite literally, when a new client walked in.

★　　★　　★

He sat back in his car and pulled out his cell phone. He never took his hard eyes off the yellow building. Punching in the number he had memorized, he waited for his boss to pick up.

"Is it done?"

"Almost. The two are taken care of," he said in his normal cold voice. He had never been hired for a hit on a woman, nevertheless two women, but he had gotten it done. Just like always.

"Then what's the problem?"

"There was a witness."

"A witness? Can they identify you?"

"Yes. The bitch tried to chase me down." He had admired her spunk, even if she showed her stupidity by chasing an armed man down.

"You know who she is?"

"Of course I do."

"Can you handle it?"

"You know I can. Her and her boyfriend live above her shop. When the timing is right, I will go in and take care of her. If he doesn't get out of the way, I will just make it look like a murder-suicide. Nothing I haven't done before." His lips twitched. He might just feel something besides boredom for this one.

"Fine. Just hurry up. I don't want any loose ends."

★　　★　　★

Cole slid his hand into hers as they walked down the street toward the cafe. Betty Jo had been very excited to see Cole in the store. Come to think about it, her traffic flow had increased as the day went on.

"I bet it was interesting growing up with all those brothers. I am kind of jealous. I always wanted siblings, but it was just me."

"Yes. It was interesting. They always wanted me to be this little girly-girl. But I always wanted to be just like them. I followed them everywhere and finally they gave in and started teaching me instead of trying to get rid of me. But then I went to design school and totally surprised everyone. I think they are torn between being proud of me and embarrassed about how I turned out."

"How did they think you would turn out?"

"I don't know. Probably something along their lines, either security or farming."

"How would you be in security?"

"Marshall always wanted me to run his company for him. I am good at business and I am good with people." She got nervous when Cole was quiet for a moment. Did he think she wasn't good enough to run a major company?

"I can see that. You would be really good at it, but I think you like being the one in charge and you have the freedom to do that with your own store." Cole opened the door at the cafe for her. She smiled as she walked in. He understood. Someone who barely knew her understood what her brothers still failed to see.

Miss Daisy gave them a wave and a wink as she shuttled from table to table taking orders. Paige made her way through the packed dining room to the only open table in the back of the room. She had hoped for a booth where she could have enough room to breathe from Cole's presence. Instead, she got a table for two pressed against the back-side wall. It was the most private table at the cafe. Cole walked around where she stood staring stupidly at the small, intimate table. He pulled out a chair and gestured for her to sit.

"How's the cutest couple in Keeneston doing?" Miss Daisy asked on a wink as she placed two menus in front of them.

"So where did you hear that we are dating?" Cole reached across the table and started tracing his fingers over the top of her hand in a motion that sent a wave of heat shooting straight from her fingers down to her, oh my!

"You know there's nothin' going on in this town I don't know about, young man. Besides Kandi stopped by for the back-to-school lunch for the PTA. Told the whole room about how you are slumming it with your help. I figured she wasn't talking about Betty

Jo, so I figured Cole used it as an excuse to stick around for a while." Miss Daisy shrugged her thin shoulders as she pulled out her pad and ever-present pen to take their drink orders before shuttling off to the kitchen.

Paige didn't bother to look down at the menu. She had it memorized. Tonight she was going to go with the grilled pimento cheese sandwich with fresh tomato and bacon. She sat quietly, looking at the people in the restaurant as Cole decided what he wanted to eat.

"How did you decide to join the FBI?" she asked when he closed his menu.

"You want the long or short version?"

"I think we have time for the long version." She looked around at the packed room and knew Miss Daisy was going to be a while.

"Well, I always wanted to be in the FBI. I was six years old when an FBI agent came to my school and told us about the agency. I played football, wide receiver, during high school and was in the National Honor Society. The combination got me noticed by some smaller schools like Sewanee, Maryville, and Rhodes in Tennessee and Georgetown and Centre in Kentucky. I narrowed it down to which ones offered me a full scholarship for academics and finally decided on Centre College down in Danville.

"I took lots of government and law classes, and they confirmed my desire to go into the FBI. My professor contacted the agency and got me an internship for the summer before my senior year. I was assigned to the Assistant Deputy Director in D.C. I was nothing more than a glorified gofer, but he let me sit in on many meetings and would even stay late to discuss the day's events with me.

"After graduating from Centre, I earned my master's in Criminal Justice from Eastern Kentucky University and was admitted to the FBI Academy. I found out later that the Assistant Deputy Director called the Director in charge of the Academy and got me in."

"That was nice of him." Paige sat back and allowed Miss Daisy to set their drinks down and take their order before hustling off for the kitchen.

"It was nice of him. It is what got me in. Turns out I didn't have enough standout qualities on my résumé and was going on the waitlist. It's very difficult to get into the Academy and he made it possible for me."

"Is that who you report to now?" Cole smiled and she knew she was right.

"Yes. When the new Director was named, he was promoted to Special Ops. He doesn't have to report to anyone unless he deems it necessary. He is going to bring the Director in on it soon."

"So, now that you have me on this date, are you going to tell me the current news?" She couldn't believe she had forgotten he had heard from his boss. She was actually having a good time talking with him.

"They ran your sketch through the system and got a hit. We don't have a real name on him, but we suspect he's behind around twenty mid-level assassinations. We're pretty sure he was hired by one or all of the New York boys to clean up the mess, as in you." Cole stared at her with his cross cop face.

"I still can't believe the owners of the largest law firm in New York City, federal and district judges, and senators could be involved in something as horrible as kidnapping, rape, and murder. I hate that Kenna and Dani were dragged into this, but at the same time, if not for them, this would still be going on. Girls would still be made to… it's too horrible to even think of." Paige felt sick just thinking of what those poor girls had to go through. She had heard the story of Kenna accidentally walking into one of the parties and witnessing her then-boyfriend, Chad Taylor, attempting to rape a woman while some of the most powerful men in the state and federal government sat back and watched. She was only now getting a taste of what Kenna and Dani must have felt that night when they ran from Chad. "Did you learn anything else?"

"Yes, thanks to Dani's tip on the bartender at the club in New York. We tracked down the bartender and found him at the gym both he and Chad belonged to. We threatened him with life in jail and he started talking instantly. Turns out he would signal Chad if there were any new young women who were unaccompanied coming into the gym or the bar. He thought Chad just had a type of girl he liked to hit on. Turns out they were probably the girls Chad would either bring to the monthly parties at the law office or he would pimp out to the judges and other VIPs who were regulars at those parties.

"The bartender led us to Chad's place. Agents are going through the place with a fine-tooth comb. It is obvious he didn't think he would ever get caught. He has all kinds of papers and pictures lying around. Even had a note that lists the fake name Judge LeMaster hid the 9-1-1 tape under. Apparently, LeMaster sent a clerk to listen to the tape. The clerk returned it to evidence, but purposely misfiled it. It can't be classified as destroying evidence. But if Chad had not written down the file it was hidden in, then we may have never have found it.

"The tape confirms everything Kenna said. You can hear her screaming for them to stop the rape and then you can hear Chad attacking Kenna. Afterwards, you actually hear Bob and Senator Bruce ordering the death of the girl.

"Normally, I think the best way is to capture criminals alive so they can pay for their crimes. But I think the best punishment he could get was to have Dani kill him. After hearing parts of the tape, no man deserved it more. Chad would never think she had it in her and that makes it all the better in my mind." Cole leaned back in his chair and ran his hand through his hair. He was obviously agitated that men like Chad and the New York boys had taken advantage of innocent women.

"I know it was hard on Dani, but I think Ahmed is helping her with his experience in killing people. Things like how to handle the nightmares and flashbacks. I think, deep down, she feels the same way you do. She knows he is dead and knows he won't ever get out of jail someday. I think it brings her a certain peace. At least it did until this. I still can't believe it happened. I didn't even know assassins existed in the real world. I thought it was just something in the movies."

"They are very real. Which is why I am so worried about you. Movies can't hurt you, but this guy can." Paige looked away from Cole and down at her napkin. She didn't want him to see she was starting to worry now that she knew all the facts.

"I see you have already run out of things to talk about." Kandi sashayed her way over to the table. Paige stifled a groan when she heard Kandi's grating voice. She raised her eyes from her napkin and almost choked with laughter.

Kandi leaned against Cole's chair in tight, barely-there shorts and an Ed Hardy t-shirt two sizes too small. She looked like she had raided a fifteen-year-old's closet.

"You know, Kandi, I have some great clothes at my store more suited to a woman of your age. You should check them out." Paige grinned and gave a slight bat of her lashes.

"Oh! Aren't you a dear? I only wear designer clothes. I know you can't afford them and probably know nothing about them. This is an Ed Hardy. This t-shirt alone costs more than you probably make in a week." Kandi turned as if Paige wasn't even sitting there and started brushing up against Cole.

"I know Don. And I know how much they cost. I have about ten of them in my closest." Paige picked up her water and took a sip as she waited for her words to make their way through all the teased hair and hairspray and into her ears.

"Oh, Paige. You're so silly. It's Ed Hardy, not Don." Paige watched as she gave Cole a look that conveyed just how stupid Kandi thought she was.

"Actually, his first name is Don and I interned with him and Christian Audigier while I was in design school. I just talked to him last week, actually." Paige took another sip of her water.

"You know, I never asked what your name is." Kandi ignored Paige, clearly not believing her. But Paige didn't care. It was enough to piss her off and that made it worth it. She'd have to dig out the picture of the three of them at New York Fashion Week just for fun.

"Cole." Cole looked at her and she just shrugged. Sometimes it was hard to detach Kandi after she leeched on to someone new.

"Oh, what a sexy name," she purred into his ear. This time Paige did laugh out loud. The look on Cole's face was priceless. A mix of repulsion and fear. "I bet you're getting real tired of her. I could always rescue you from such a boring girlfriend." It looked to Paige as if Kandi managed to pump up her breast size again as she leaned closer to Cole's face.

"She's good at rescuing things. She has built-in life preservers." At Kandi's shocked face, she put on her best smile. "Don't worry, they look natural." Kandi narrowed her eyes at her, executed a perfect hair flip, and walked back to the table filled with her minions. The same minions that helped terrorize Paige in high school.

"She's scary." Cole gave a quick shiver of his body as proof.

"Thanks for trying to make me feel better. I know I am nothing compared to her physically, but I like to think I am a better person on the inside."

"I think you're much better than her, inside and out." Cole reached across the table and pulled her hand into his. "What happened between you two? Has she always been like this?"

"Yes. She was the popular kid in school. First to have a car of her own, head cheerleader, dated anyone she wanted... Her last name was Chase, and it was the school joke that it was fun to 'chase Kandi,' but even better to catch her. I, on the other hand, was the tomboy on the rifle team who was a well-known virgin."

"How could that be well-known?" Cole laughed.

"You've met my brothers, right? They made sure I was off limits. While it made them feel better, it made me a social outcast. At the beginning of my senior year, I somehow got the attention of the starting quarterback, Bill Rawlings. We started dating and my popularity shot up, not that I cared. We were the perfect couple, or so I thought. He earned a walk-on spot with the University of Kentucky football team and I was going to go to the design program there. We planned on getting engaged the night of our senior prom and then getting married during the summer before football season started." She stopped when she saw Cole raise his eyebrow at the mention of getting married.

"I know, we were really young. But in a small town like this, lots of people get married right out of high school. Anyway, prom rolls around and we get engaged, but as we are about to head out to the after-party at one of the farms, Kandi comes staggering over and says it's only fitting for the prom king to escort the prom queen to the party. Kandi's merry minions circle around me and take me off to the party. I am there an hour and Bill still hadn't shown up, so I just went home."

"Ouch. He and Kandi?"

"I'll get to that. So, he stops by first thing the next morning and said she got sick and he had to take her home, blah blah blah. In my naïveté, I believed him. At graduation two months later, Bill pulls me aside and confesses to an affair with Kandi. He tells me he wants to stay together and work things out. I forgive him and agree to it before he finishes his confession. Kandi was two months pregnant and he wanted her to live near us in Lexington until she had the baby so he could 'do the right thing' and look after her."

"No. No man can be that stupid."

Paige smiled. Somehow it didn't hurt anymore as she told Cole about her last and only relationship. "Yes, yes they can be. So, I immediately withdrew from UK and applied for school in Los Angeles. I headed out two weeks later and didn't come back for three years. So, that's my embarrassing relationship story." Paige put down the napkin she had torn to shreds.

"Well, what happened to Bill and Kandi?"

"They got married right after their son was born. She didn't want to be fat in her pictures. They are still married. I don't really know more than that."

"If I am honest, I am glad it happened. It means you get to be my girlfriend now." He winked and she laughed.

Chapter Six

Paige couldn't remember ever having such a great time on a date. She had been on a lot of first dates and none of them had been this relaxed and fun. Her high was brought down when she realized it didn't matter. It wasn't a real first date. It was all for show. Paige and Cole approached the shop in a peaceful silence. He took her key and opened the front door.

She walked in and the hair on the back of her neck stood up. She looked around carefully. Nothing seemed to be missing. She looked closer and saw that all the displays were in order. She couldn't figure it out. It just felt as if something was out of place. She slowly walked up the stairs behind Cole. Maybe it was just her imagination, but he seemed tense, too.

He opened her door and Chuck walked out with his tail slowly wagging. He approached the top of the steps ready for his nighttime walk. Cole walked through her apartment, checking each room before coming out with Chuck's leash in his hand.

"It's all clear, but something seems off."

"I know." She looked around the shop as she walked down the stairs. "But, nothing seems to be missing."

"Come on. Let's take Chuck for his nighttime walk. Maybe things will be clearer in the morning." Cole snapped Chuck's flexi-leash in place and opened the door for her. Paige walked out with Chuck glued to her side. Cole shut the door and locked it before turning toward Paige.

"Where do you normally walk him?"

"We go around the block to the park behind the store. Then we just go up the stairs and into the apartment from the back," she said as they headed down the sidewalk.

"You know, I had a really good time tonight."

"You don't have to say that. I know it wasn't real for you."

"Was it real for you?" Cole asked, his voice barely above a whisper.

Before she could answer, Chuck froze. She felt the vibration of his growl running up the leash before she could hear it. As soon as Cole heard the growl, a gun appeared in his right hand and he stepped in front of her to shield her from whatever was in the park. Chuck pulled on his leash and let out a deep bark. Paige looked around and didn't see anyone. That didn't stop Chuck from pulling at the end of his leash. He desperately wanted to get at whoever was behind the trees.

Her first instinct was to run and hide behind Cole. But her curiosity won out and she edged her way out from behind him to stare into the unknown darkness of the park. Chuck's growls grew more and more agitated as he lunged forward again. His chocolate brown hair stood on end down his back.

"Come out with your hands up," Cole called into the darkness. Silence echoed around them as they waited for the person to come out.

She felt him tense and raise his gun when she heard the leaves rustle. Someone was coming toward them. Her heart skipped a beat as the rustling grew louder. Chuck was frantically pulling on his leash and Paige had to use both hands to hold him back.

"Slowly now. Hands up in the air so I can see them!" Cole yelled out as the large shrub in front of them started to move. Cole reached out with his left arm and pushed her behind him one last time. She felt him freeze and slowly moved to look over his shoulder.

"Oh shit. Run!" Chuck lunged and broke free from Paige's grasp. Paige screamed as Cole grabbed her and shoved her away from the trees. But it was too late.

The putrid smell permeated the heavy humid air and clung to them. The lack of breeze caused the noxious gas to envelope them. Paige felt tears stream down her face and her lungs constricted as she gasped for fresh air.

"You were real handy with that gun, Cole. Good thing you were here to protect me from that skunk." Paige coughed some more and tried to drag in a breath of fresh air as they staggered away from ground zero. "You did order his hands up. Hands, tail… same thing to a skunk, I guess," she laughed in between fits of coughing.

"Hopefully, Chuck made it worthwhile and killed that damn thing." Cole bent over at his waist and coughed. "Here's the mighty hunter now." Chuck came running back over toward them with his tail wagging, skunk safely in his grasp spraying everything in range.

"Oh, Chuck!" Paige backed up, holding up her hands as if to defend herself from the pissed-off skunk Chuck was bringing to her. Thinking it a game, Chuck wagged his tail and trotted after her.

"No! Chuck, put him down," Cole said in his most authoritative voice. Chuck turned his bright brown eyes toward Cole and ran over toward him. "No!" Cole tried to get away, but it was too late. Chuck had gotten close enough for the skunk to have a direct shot at Cole.

Paige laughed but that caused Chuck's attention to focus back on her. He began to run happily toward her, tail wagging, with his prize. Paige backed up, but Chuck just broke out into a run. There was no way she was going to let him near her. She ducked behind a large ash tree as Chuck got near. Looking up, she grabbed the lowest branch and swung upward.

She looked five feet down at Chuck and hoped the skunk couldn't spray her up in the perch. Chuck pranced around the tree showing her his new toy as Cole tried to get his breath back from his spraying. His eyes were bloodshot and he swiped at the involuntary tears running down his cheeks.

"Chuck, put down the skunk and I will get you a big treat," Paige cooed to him. Chuck just wagged his tail and sat down. The skunk seemed to have given up and lowered his tail. There appeared to be a limit on how much they could spray. When the skunk stopped struggling, Chuck quickly lost interest and opened his mouth. The skunk fell from his mouth, turned his back to Chuck, and sprayed him directly in the face. Who knew? Maybe they did have an unlimited supply. Chuck yelped and covered his eyes with his paws. He rubbed his face in the grass as the skunk ran for the shrubs. Paige could have sworn the skunk smiled. Chuck looked up at her, sneezed, and thumped his tail against the grass.

"Come on, let's get this smell washed off." Cole strode over to the tree and smiled up at her. She laid her head against the tree trunk and laughed. She had a fake boyfriend who was turning out to be perfect. And here she was, skunked. And he just smiled that very sexy smile while his eyes danced at her.

Paige ran up the rickety back steps and unlocked the kitchen door. She looked over the rail to where Cole was hooking up the hose. Chuck sulked a few feet away at the sight of the hose. She rushed into her kitchen and opened the pantry door. She found five cans of tomato sauce and put them into a plastic grocery bag to carry downstairs. As she closed the door, she caught another whiff of herself and knew her house was going to stink. She ran back down the stairs and laughed at Chuck's tucked tail and the glare he was casting at Cole.

"Here's all the tomato sauce I have." She put the bags down and started opening the cans as Cole hosed him down.

She poured the first can over him and was surprised when the smell actually lessened. By the fifth can, the smell on Chuck became acceptable. Paige sprayed him with some of her locally made spritzer to cover any lingering smells. She looked down at her shirt and cringed. She and Cole were sopping wet and smelled horrible.

"My house is going to smell for weeks."

"I don't think it would be a good idea to bring our clothes inside right now. We should leave them out here to air out and then see if we can salvage them after a couple of washings." Cole looked down at his shirt, shrugged, and pulled it off.

Oh my. Paige ran her eyes over his bare chest and abs. She found herself unable to tear her gaze away from him. That is, until his hand went to the button of his jeans.

"What are you doing?!" She gasped and dragged her eyes past his defined abs and muscled chest to his laughing eyes.

"I told you. We shouldn't go upstairs with our clothes on since they are holding the majority of the bad smell."

Paige's mouth fell open as she watched him slide his jeans off. He stood confidently in her backyard wearing nothing but a pair of black boxer briefs as he hung his clothes up on the railing. He turned back around and gave her another bone-melting smile.

"What? You're not wearing anything under that sexy little dress?"

"Huh?"

"Take off your clothes, Paige." His voice had dropped a little as he walked toward her, his eyes never leaving hers.

"Okay," she said as though she were in a trance. She untied the red scarf from her waist and let it drop to the ground. Cole slowly slid his hands down her back and unzipped her dress.

They were standing so close her lips brushed his neck as her dress fell to the ground. It was a good thing she shaved this morning, she thought as she felt Cole's fingers wrap around the back of her neck. Cole stepped forward and her lace-covered breasts pressed against his wet chest. Her body hummed with his nearness and the only thing she could think about was how much she wanted his hands on her. Cole leaned forward as he pulled her closer with his hand on her neck and gently kissed her forehead. Huh?

"I'll let you have first dibs on the shower." He stepped back and started to pick up her clothes.

Paige stood rooted to the ground. No, there was no way she misinterpreted that. He was being all sexy and then a kiss to the forehead? She watched as he hung her clothes on the railing and suddenly felt very self-conscious standing there in her underwear when he clearly didn't find her irresistible. She ran up the cold metal stairs with Chuck right behind her before the shock wore off and the tears of rejection started. Cole said nothing and turned his back to the rail as she ran up it.

Paige slammed the bathroom door closed as the tears burst forth. Chuck whined and sat down on the mat in front of the bathtub, clearly upset with her tears. Paige finished getting undressed and climbed into the big bathtub and shower. She tried to wash the smell from her skin and calm down. She had read it all wrong. He was just doing his job. They weren't really dating. She knew that.

For all the effort her brothers had put into protecting her, she was still green when it came to men. She could out-shoot them, out-drive them, and out-play them in poker. But when it came to relationships, she was lost. Her one and only serious relationship was with Bill and he had left a sour taste in her mouth. She had dated in L.A., but never for more than a month or two. Then, for some reason, she started falling for this guy she couldn't stand only days before. Maybe it was all stress from the events over the past couple of days. That was it. It was just a byproduct of stress. Feeling better, she got out of the shower and dried off. She slid into an old pair of boxers and a UK basketball shirt and climbed into bed.

Paige woke up the following morning in a horrible mood. She knew from the second her eyes opened that she should just stay in bed. She had tossed and turned all night dreaming of different versions of the previous night. Versions that did not end with a friendly kiss on the forehead. As a result, she was wound up with no way to release the energy. It wasn't a real relationship after all. Maybe if she found someone else she wouldn't be so high-strung.

She got up and curled her hair. She put on a little make-up and some nude lip gloss. She found the short denim skirt Cole hated and put on a tight, black lace tank top with a low boat neck. She dug around her closet and came out with some cute wedge sandals that added a couple inches to her five-seven height and smiled. She looked good and nothing soothed the pain of rejection better than knowing that.

Paige heard Cole in the shower as she walked downstairs to open her shop. She loved turning on the lights and turning the sign to Open every morning. It reminded her of how hard she had worked to get there. Moments after opening the store, customers started to wander in. She had already made a couple of sales of her new ribbon hair ties when Cole came downstairs. She kept focused on restocking the shelves but saw him stop and stare at her. Good. Let him suffer. They worked around each other as if they were two tigers trapped in a small cage all morning. Customers gave them odd looks as they worked very hard to ignore each other.

"What is the matter with you today?" Cole whispered while Miss Lily's neighbor, Edna, shopped around the bridal section.

"Nothing. I am having a pretty good day actually. Why?"

"Well, you're just being weird."

"Weird? Um, okay." Paige turned and walked toward her customer. "Edna. Is there anything I can help you with?"

"There sure is. I need a gift for my granddaughter's wedding. Do you have any recommendations on what young people like nowadays?"

"I found the personalized champagne glasses for the wedding toast to be very popular. Although, you'd have to give them to her before the wedding."

"Great idea. I'll do that."

Paige grabbed a box of the crystal champagne glasses and headed to the store's front. She stepped around Cole at the register and rung Edna up.

"Just tell me their names and the etcher will have them decorated by the end of the week."

"Perfect! It's Bella and Justin Thurmond. Thanks, Paige." Edna looked around the store some more. "You know, don't ring it up quite yet. I want to look at a new hat for church. Lily Rae got one last week and everyone gushed over it. I can't have her showing me up, now can I?"

"No, ma'am." Paige grinned as she watched Edna walk back to the hat room. She was about to show her some of the new hats when the bell rang over the front door again.

Paige looked at the door and saw a handsome man in a black suit and blue tie walk in. He looked uncomfortable as he looked around her shop. She knew that look. It was the same look her brothers gave whenever they walked into her shop. She smiled and was about to ask him if she could help when Cole cut in front of her.

"I'll help him," Cole told her as he walked from behind the counter. "Hi. Welcome to Southern Charms. Can I help you find anything?" Cole had a smile on his face, but Paige easily read the defensive stance.

"Yeah. My buddy from college is getting married this weekend. I need a wedding gift. Any ideas?" Paige tried not to laugh at the look on Cole's face. He looked as panicked as the customer.

"Is it the Thurmond wedding?" Paige asked as she walked around the counter.

"Yes." The man smiled at Paige and she smiled back. He was rather handsome. Not as ruggedly so as Cole, but more business handsome.

"The grandmother of the bride just picked out these crystal champagne glasses. You could always pick out a set of crystal wine glasses and I can have them engraved with a T. You could pick them up Friday."

"That would be perfect. Thanks for your help. Are you going to the wedding?" he asked Paige as she wrapped up the glasses and wrote the instructions for the engraver.

"No. I am sure it will be fun, though."

"Well, if you want, you could…"

"Thanks for stopping by Southern Charms. I apologize for being rude, but Paige is needed in the back." Cole cut in, glaring at them both while trying to paste on a smile.

"For what?" Paige asked.

The second the man turned to leave, Cole grabbed her hand in his and started to pull her toward the small office under the stairs.

"Cole, what are you doing? Didn't it ever occur to you I might want to go out on a date with someone?" Paige tried to drag her feet, but Cole just pulled her along.

He was muttering something about crossing a line and his duty, but she couldn't put it all together. He opened the door and pushed her in before him. The second the door closed, he had her up against the door. His mouth was on hers. It wasn't like in her dreams. It was fierce, primal, and hot. He grabbed her hips and ground them against his growing erection as she wrapped her arms around his neck. She lifted her leg and he put it around his waist. He picked her up, his tongue never leaving her mouth as they tried to satisfy their thirst for each other.

Cole moaned and gave her one last slow kiss before setting her down. They were both panting and Paige could have sworn she was seeing stars. She leaned against one of the shelves and tried to slow her heart rate as Cole tucked his shirt back into his jeans.

"Maybe that will answer why you are not going out on a date with him." Cole turned and walked out the door, leaving Paige staring after him.

What the hell just happened? Whatever it was, it left her feeling both dazed and yearning for more. She certainly hadn't done him enough justice in her dreams. Paige stood up to straighten her outfit and fix her hair. She took a deep breath and opened the door. Edna was standing across the hall in the hat room with a sneaky smile on her face. Oh no. Edna was the one of the biggest gossips in town.

"Oh, that was so romantic. Young love is so wonderful." Edna clasped the small white hat with blue ribbon and white daisies on it to her chest and sighed.

"That hat will be perfect for you." Paige ignored the love talk and found a hatbox for Edna.

"I remember the days when Richard and I were like that. Sneaking off to the nearest coat closet to get frisky, God rest his soul." Edna had a faraway look in her eyes and Paige definitely didn't want to use the words *love, marriage,* and *frisky* when talking about Cole. It was bad enough she was already thinking kissing, hands, and naked bodies.

"Here you go, Edna. Just come in on Friday to pick up the glasses." Paige handed her the receipt and the hatbox. She needed to get out of there and fast. She needed to take a deep breath and think about just what happened.

After Edna left, she grabbed Chuck's leash from under the counter and shouted up to Cole that she was taking Chuck for a walk. Before Cole could make his way downstairs to stop her, she bolted out the front door.

This isn't real. This isn't real. She kept up her mantra for the first block. The hot July sun was beating down on her, but she didn't notice. Paige looked up and didn't see anything, but she could have sworn she had seen someone in her peripheral vision. She shook it off and kept walking down Main Street away from town. She was just going to walk to the elementary school and then turn back.

She just didn't understand this newfound chemistry they had together. He was a neat freak and she was kind of sloppy. He was picky and controlling, and she was, too! They bickered over little things, like the fact she ate on the run as opposed to cooking a meal. But, at the same time, she had been enjoying herself with him... in more ways than one.

She stopped when she heard a footfall behind her. Chuck growled and they both turned around. It made her worry even more when no one was there. Was she going crazy? No, Chuck seemed to have heard something, too. She heard some noise, now coming from the direction she had been walking. She turned back up the street and saw a couple of mothers pushing strollers and some young kids running around them. They were coming from the school playground and were walking back into town.

Something just didn't feel right. Did the mothers scare off whoever was behind her? Chuck hadn't moved from where he was looking. She followed his stare to the alley running along the feed store and butcher shop, less than a block from where she stood. Maybe she was jumping at ghosts, but she wasn't about to find out. She looked at the street and when the slow-moving pick-up truck towing hay passed by, she ran across. She looked around again but didn't see anything or anyone out of the ordinary. What really worried her was the fact she could still feel the vibrations of a low growl from Chuck. She walked as quickly as she could back toward town. She could see her shop across the street when a man stepped in front of her. She screamed and jumped back. Chuck growled and barked as he stood guard.

"That's not usually the reception I get when I run into a hot woman like you."

"Henry! Oh, you scared me." She took a deep breath and looked around. She saw she was at the alley leading back to the parking lot behind the law office. She had been so intent on looking across the street that she hadn't noticed what was right in front of her.

"Again, not the normal reception I get."

"I am sorry. I just thought I was being followed and it freaked me out." Paige looked back to where the moms were passing the feed store. There was no sign of the boogeyman.

"It's okay, really. You want me to walk you back to your boyfriend? You know, make sure you get there safe?"

"Henry. How did you know Cole's my boyfriend?"

"Easy. Edna told John she saw you all go at in the office. No one who wasn't dating you would be stupid enough to do that."

Paige groaned. If Edna was the second-biggest gossip, then John Wolfe was the first. Between the two of them, most of the state would know by now that she got kissed, and kissed well, in her office all of thirty minutes ago.

"What do you mean 'stupid enough'?"

"Hello? Did you forget who your brothers are? I mean, you're great and all, but they're a wee bit overprotective. Why do you think I have never hit on you?"

Paige couldn't decide whether that was a good thing or not. It was nice not being hit on by Henry, but finding a guy who wasn't afraid of her brothers was close to impossible. Great. Her brothers were going to make her an old maid.

"Thanks, Henry. If you just watch me, then I will head back to the store and let Cole know what's going on." Paige waved bye and ran across the street.

Chapter Seven

Paige sat on the couch in her living room and watched Cole pace back and forth. The conversation had not gone well. Cole had first called the sheriff's department and then her brothers. Red's men were already outside looking around. Miles and Marshall were in Lexington and would get here soon. Ugh, a safety lecture from Cole, and then her brothers. As if an FBI agent wasn't enough, her brothers' years of military intelligence were going to be even worse. It was bad enough when they were kids. But then the U.S. went and trained them to interrogate terrorists. This was really going to suck.

"Paige, did you hear what I said?"

"Hmm?" Paige snapped her focus back onto the irate Cole. Wait a minute, she thought. She watched him a couple seconds more as he ran his hand through his dark hair, pacing back and forth. He wasn't irate. He was worried.

"Agent Parker! We found some shoe tracks in the mud of the flower beds under the downstairs windows out back." Deputy Smalls reported. Smalls was around six-seven and a good three hundred fifty pounds. So, the obvious nickname in Keeneston was Smalls. She remembered Howard Brown, also known as Smalls, from high school. He was a senior when she was a freshman. He entered the sheriff's department as soon as he graduated and was a great guy living his dream.

"Are you finally going to listen to me, Paige? You're in danger. Please, just let me protect you."

Paige nodded. Maybe she wasn't as aware as she should be. She had shrugged last night off as just a weird feeling. But that, on top of knowing she had been followed and knowing someone had been looking in the windows, was enough to freak her out. She looked up from where she had laced her hands and saw Cole sit down next to her.

"I'm sorry about snapping at you. I came downstairs and you were gone. I was frantic. I ran outside and saw you walking back toward the shop. I came inside and watched to make sure you got here safely. I just don't know what I would do if something happened to you." He slid his hand over hers.

She raised her eyes to his and saw the concern there. The line between fake and real started to blur. His hand brushed against her cheek as he pulled her head slowly toward his.

"So, the rumors are true then."

Paige jumped back and saw that Cole was already standing in front of her with his gun drawn.

"Jesus, Miles. Haven't you ever heard of knocking? Hey, Marshall, you bring the equipment?" Cole holstered his gun, but continued to stand in front of her.

"I think we need to have a talk, Cole."

"I agree. Your sister is in danger. The sheriff's department found footprints out back. I think we need to hide cameras on the roof and on the downstairs windows in case he peeks in again."

"That's not the talk I was referring to," Miles ground out.

"I know. But, I am pretty sure Paige is an adult and can decide who she wants to kiss. It's none of your concern." Cole placed his hands on his hips and stared Miles down.

"It *is* our concern. She's our sister and we look out for her." Marshall stepped up beside Miles and the stare-down continued.

"Really? Does she interrupt you when you are with women?"

"Of course not," Marshall laughed. "But what's your point?"

"The point is to give her the same courtesy. She trusts your opinion enough not to question who you are with. Why don't you extend her the same courtesy?"

"We'll talk about this later, Parker," Miles said.

"Anytime, Davies."

Paige was left upstairs with Chuck as her brothers and Cole installed the security cameras around her property. She picked up the *Keeneston Journal* and froze at the sight of McKenna and Danielle's side-by-side obituaries. She read the articles by Marianne and had to keep telling herself it wasn't real. Marianne really did do a great job. She had quotes from the Rose sisters, Mo, Will, Danielle's parents, and the Ashtons.

Paige couldn't help the feeling that all the lines in her life were blurring. Her fake relationship with Cole was starting to feel more and more real. Her friends' fake deaths were starting to feel more and more real. Paige stood up and started to pace the room. She didn't like the feeling of not being in control. The feeling that she was starting to become confused on what was real and what was fake.

"Hey. What's the matter?" Cole asked as he walked into the room and saw her pacing.

"I saw the obits."

"Marianne did a great job."

"She sure did. But, Cole, I need to see Dani and Kenna right now." Paige stopped pacing in front of him and looked him in the eyes.

"I am sorry. It would give their cover away if anyone sees you going there."

"I will do it without you then." She took a deep breath and let it out slowly. "Cole, it's getting to me. Our fake relationship suddenly seems real. My friends' fake death suddenly seems real. I just need to see them," she pleaded.

"Okay. I have an idea." Cole picked up his phone and walked into the kitchen.

★   ★   ★

Paige slipped on Dinky's extra uniform and pinned her hair up and under the SHERIFF ball cap. Dinky and Noodle were stretched out in front of the television while Cole changed into Noodle's uniform in the bathroom.

"Thanks for helping me out, guys."

"No problem. Just tell the gals we say hi," Noodle said in his Southern twang.

"Ready to go, Paige?" Cole asked as he walked out of the bathroom. Paige nodded as she stared at him and swallowed. There was just something about a good-looking man in uniform.

"Okay. This will be real easy. Just walk out and get into the passenger side of the cruiser. Pull the cap low. Walk slowly and confidently.

Paige and Cole headed downstairs. She followed Cole out the door and went straight to the door of the cruiser. Cole meandered through town for twenty minutes until he declared them free of any tails.

The trip to the hospital was silent. Paige was too confused to want to talk about anything. She was still trying to work through her feelings. As they approached the hospital, she started bouncing her legs in anticipation of seeing her two friends.

"It's okay, Paige. They are recovering and are safe."

"I'm just anxious to see them." Paige opened the door to the car as soon as they stopped. She hurried to the back entrance where Cole flashed his badge and got them in.

"They are over here." Cole strode through the hospital wings until he reached the maternity ward.

"What are we doing here?"

"It's where they are staying. The maternity ward is constantly monitored with video, heightened security guard presence, and a check-in reception area. It would be very difficult for someone to find them here." Cole flashed his badge and was instantly surrounded by security and a nurse who was clearly one of Mo's undercover guards. "Cole Parker, FBI. This is Paige Davies. Here are our IDs." He handed over his badge and her driver's license. He just shrugged when he saw her glaring at him. He must have gone in her purse and gotten her license while she was changing. After being cleared, they were led to Kenna's room first.

"Go ahead, I want to talk to the doctors. I will be in shortly." Cole brushed back a piece of Paige's hair that had come down from under her cap and gave her a slight smile before turning toward the nurses' station.

"Kenna!" Paige squealed as she launched herself at her friend, only remembering to pull back at the last minute.

"Paige. I am so glad you are here!" Kenna grabbed her hand and squeezed.

"How are you feeling? How's the baby?"

"We are both doing great. I am due in early February." Kenna was still in a tank top. Her right shoulder was covered in gauze while her arm was in a sling. Her auburn hair was braided in pigtails and she looked happier than Paige had ever seen her.

"Actually, I am glad you stopped by. Kenna and I have been talking about what to do about the football team," Will said as he stood up so Paige could sit in the chair next to the bed.

"What about the team?"

"After all this and knowing we have a baby on the way, well, I am not sure I want to coach next year. I may just volunteer part-time. But I don't want to hang the boys out to dry. The only way I will step down is if Cade will take the head-coaching job. Do you think he would consider it?" Will asked.

"Of course he would! He loves it."

Will looked so relieved. Paige couldn't wait to tell her brother.

"But don't tell him yet. I am still trying to convince him I will be fine. I know he loves coaching and I don't want him to stop for me," Kenna told her.

"Okay. I'll let you all decide and then you can tell him the news."

"So, a more interesting question is… what's going on with you and Cole? I heard you all went at it in some closet. Nice." Kenna winked at her and Paige felt her face color.

"It's complicated. It's a fake relationship that has real qualities. And, how could you possibly know that?"

"We get so many calls a day on Will's cell phone. Apparently Edna ran into John on the way home and by the time she made it to Miss Lily's, John had already called. Edna was pissed. Anyway, all I have to say is it took you all long enough. You two have been shooting off sparks for months now."

Paige didn't know how to respond to Kenna. Sparks? Months? She was saved from having to say anything when Cole walked in.

"Well, I have good news. You're being discharged tomorrow." Cole smiled and shook hands with Will.

"Discharged to where?" Kenna asked. "Not that I can't wait to get out of the hospital."

"To a safe house."

"Oh great. Recovering in some tiny cheap motel. Maybe the hospital is sounding better," Kenna joked.

"Actually, I am putting you all up at my house. You'll have more room. It won't be anywhere on the books or use any FBI funds so there is no way the shooter will find out." Cole paused for a second and opened the folder he had been carrying. "Now that you're feeling better and not under any pain medication, can you look this over and sign it? It's your affidavit." Cole handed her the document and stepped back.

"Do you still need Dani's?" Kenna asked as she started reading. Paige wanted to laugh at how fast her lawyer mask fell into place.

"Got it before you came back from your honeymoon. We also got Whitney's back when we arrested her at the Derby. Your affidavit is the last one we need before we can simultaneously move on your old boss, Bob Greendale, and Whitney's father, Senator Bruce. Chad confessed to Bruce's men dumping the bodies on Bob's swamp property. We have narrowed down which property. After a sweep of that property, we expect to find at least one body. The way Chad talked before Dani shot him, there could be dozens more."

Cole continued, "We will have men sitting on the rest of the ring. Once we have evidence of a crime, mainly the murders of those women, we'll move in and arrest the whole group. My boss will then fly in from DC and interview them personally. There will be no pulling rank on younger officers here."

"How long until this all goes down?" Kenna asked as she turned the page and continued reading.

"As soon as I get your affidavit, I will fax it and they will start mobilizing tonight. They will probably coordinate the watchers at first light. When they are in place, we will serve the warrants on Bob and Bruce. I expect it to start tomorrow mid-morning with the whole group brought in by the afternoon." The way Cole stood and the way his eyes were shining, Paige could tell he wanted to be there. After all, he was the lead on the case and he should be there.

Kenna just nodded as she continued reading the document. She turned the page and Paige could tell Cole wished Kenna would hurry up. He was running his thumb along his fingertips, giving away his excitement to get the warrants served. Kenna just held out her hand and Cole placed a pen in it. She made a couple of small notations and initialed them. Then she signed the document.

"There. Go do your thing, Agent." Kenna handed the document to Cole. "Dani is next door planning her wedding. Make him take you there before he goes running off to New York."

"Oh, I am not going to New York," Cole told her as he went to open the door.

"Why not? You're the lead on the case." Kenna voiced just what Paige had been thinking.

"I am staying here to protect Paige. There is still someone out to kill her, as we both know after today."

"Today?" Kenna asked. She turned her courtroom glare and Paige shriveled under it.

"I kinda had this feeling I was being followed. Then they found footprints under my back windows."

"Why didn't you tell us? Are you okay?" Kenna had an amazing ability to flip in between lawyer mode and caring friend, much like Cole with his cop mode.

"I am fine. Marshall is putting in a state-of-the-art security system. Nothing for you to worry about."

"She's right. Just focus on getting better. Red will be here tomorrow to transport you to my house in an ambulance. I am sure Mo will send some of his men ahead to scope things out once I talk to him."

"Okay. Be careful and call Will's phone if you need anything."

Paige walked out the door Cole was holding open and smiled. Her friend was happy and her baby healthy. She looked at Cole and gave him a small smile, too.

"What?"

"Thanks for bringing me."

Cole slung his arm around her shoulder and steered her to the room one door up. "Anything for you." He lowered his head and gave her a quick kiss on the cheek before knocking on the door. Mo opened the door and Paige smiled at her friend's fiancé. He was in a three-piece black suit and looked like he was in a boardroom, not a hospital. She had never seen him out of a suit, but Dani swore she had seen him in jeans once.

"Paige. Cole. Danielle will be so happy to see you." Mo displayed calm grace as usual. Not even a shooting could overshadow his royal upbringing.

"Hi, Mo. How are you both doing?" Mo opened the door for her and Dani smiled when she saw them.

"We are doing well. The chest tube comes out tomorrow and then we get to go home in a week or two," Dani answered for him. "But, that's nothing compared to the gossip I am hearing."

"What gossip and how are you hearing anything?" Cole asked. Paige rolled her eyes at the cop mode he had switched into and then tried to signal Dani to shut up. She gently shook her head, held her finger to her lips. When Dani ignored her, she cut her finger across her throat and Dani just smiled. "Oh, all about some hot make-out action in the closet of Southern Charms. You couldn't even wait until poor Miss Edna picked out her hat, could you, Cole?"

Paige buried her head in her hands and groaned but not before seeing Cole smile. She thought he would be embarrassed but instead he seemed proud.

"When the mood strikes. At least our parents didn't walk in on us."

"Hey. I am sick, you can't bring that up. It's against the rules," Dani said as she tried not to laugh.

"How are you feeling?" Paige asked once Dani calmed down.

"Pretty uncomfortable. I can't wait for the chest tube to come out. However, Mo and I have gotten a lot of wedding planning done. Speaking of which, Paige, would you be my bridesmaid?"

"Of course I will!"

"Wonderful! We were thinking December seventh. It will be Mo's thirty-fifth birthday. Figured to give one little barb at my future father-in-law for his inane contract forcing Mo to marry by then." Dani smiled and held out her hand for Mo. "Although, I must say, your parents have been great. They are hanging out with my parents and they sneak in to see me every day. The moms are even planning a bridal tea for when I am recovered."

"That's great. I bet you are very relieved it all worked out." Paige smiled and felt the same twinge of jealousy she had felt seeing Will and Kenna in love just moments ago. It was a happy jealousy, though. She just hoped she'd be as fortunate as her two friends with love.

"Cole, fill us in on the investigation," Mo asked, but it came out as more of a demand.

"Yes, sir!" Cole joked. Mo gave a sheepish smile as Cole continued, "Kenna just signed her affidavit. Along with Whitney's and the two taped affidavits I have of Dani, the FBI will move into action tonight and if we have enough people, the whole operation will be done by tomorrow afternoon."

"Enough people?" Mo asked.

"Yes. Lots of manpower for this operation, but at the same time it has to be manpower we trust. We need enough agents to sit on every member of the group while two teams go through Greendale and Bruce's properties. We don't want to tip anyone off and send them running for the airport," Cole explained.

"Take Ahmed and some of his security. We have a full team here. I can easily spare ten men. One of my men can assist one agent, thus keeping the chances of a leak low while providing all the manpower you need."

"Thanks, Mo. Give me a second to call my boss and I'll let you know in a minute." Cole opened the glass door and stepped out into the hallway.

"Girl, about damn time." Dani smiled as she leaned back into her pillows and reached for Mo's hand.

"About time for what?" Paige had a feeling this conversation was not going in a direction she wanted.

"About time you finally made a move on that man. You two have been eyeing each other for as long as I've been here. I thought you two would explode if you didn't get it on soon."

"Yes, it has been very uncomfortable for us. We are so glad you both realized what all of us were seeing," Mo chimed in.

Oh no. Mo, too? How did everyone see something that she was only starting to get glimpses of? Before she could react to the fact everyone just assumed she was now in a relationship, the object of said relationship strode back into the room.

"It's a go. Can your men be up there by seven in the morning?" Cole asked Mo.

"No problem." Mo was already pulling out his cell phone and punching in numbers.

Paige's attention was drawn to Dani as she yawned. Paige took in the yawn and the drooping eyes and knew it was time to get going. Dani needed her rest. She caught Cole's eye and gave a nod toward the bed. Cole got the message and moved over to her. She couldn't help but lean into him when he put his arm around her shoulder.

"I better get Paige back to the shop before she's missed. Feel better, Dani." Cole gave Dani a smile and shook Mo's hand before stepping out the door.

Paige gave Dani and Mo a quick hug. She tried to think of anything but the car ride home with Cole and these feelings that were starting to surface.

Chapter Eight

Cole was quiet on the ride home. Paige tried to keep her eyes out the front window but kept noticing her gaze was continually drawn to Cole. She tried to convince herself that he was an arrogant jerk who liked to tell her everything she did wrong, but the argument sounded weak even to her.

Cole parked the cruiser in front of her store again and she checked to make sure her hair was still tucked under her hat before stepping out and trying to casually walk into her home. She found Dinky and Noodle riveted to the new show about city folk being taught how to noodle catfish with their hands.

"Hey. How did it go?" Noodle asked in his slow country twang.

"Good. They're both doing great considering what they have had to go through." Paige took a seat on the couch and took off her hat. "Thanks for letting us borrow these."

"No problem. Here's a manual Marshall left for you on how to use the security system." Noodle showed her the four-inch thick binder Marshall had left behind. There was no way she'd ever learn how to use it. Why couldn't there just be an on/off button?

Paige and Cole gave their borrowed uniforms back to Noodle and Dinky, fed Chuck, and ate some leftover pizza while they finished watching the noodling show.

"Want to stay here while I take Chuck for a walk?" Cole asked as he picked up Chuck's spare leash from the counter. Chuck's long leash and collar had been trashed after the skunking.

"No. I think I will come with you. I enjoy walking outside at night when the streets are quiet."

Cole handed the leash to Paige as he set the new alarm and locked the door behind them. Without asking, he took the leash from Paige. His hand caressed hers as he took it. They were only a block from the shop when Cole stopped.

"What's wrong?" Paige asked as she turned to Cole.

"Chuck's growling. He senses something ahead of us." Before he could tell her more, Chuck barked and lunged free. "Shit! Paige, go back to the store and keep that alarm set." Cole took off down the street calling after Chuck. Paige listened and heard two sets of footsteps. Cole's and whoever Chuck had sensed. It was enough to trigger her fight-or-flight mechanism.

Paige ran back to the store, disarmed the alarm, went in, and then turned it back on. She went to the window and tried to look down the street to catch a glimpse of Cole and Chuck. She started to pace back and forth when she didn't see them, glancing out the window every time she passed it. Her heart was pounding and her hands sweating. She realized it wasn't out of fear for her safety, but fear for Cole. He had run straight into danger for her.

She jumped when she heard a creak from a floorboard. She grabbed a candlestick and crept slowly toward the kitchen, holding her breath as she quietly snuck forward. Paige took a deep breath as she leaned against the wall next to the door leading into the kitchen. She tried to listen to see if she heard him again, but the only thing she could hear was her wildly beating heart. She jumped through the door with the candlestick raised and prepared to attack.

Her eyes darted around the kitchen. They froze, along with her breathing, as a shadow passed by the kitchen window on the outside staircase. She watched in horror as she saw the door handle turn. She raised the candlestick and involuntarily stepped backwards into the small kitchen table. The handle rattled again before the shadow banged loudly on it.

"Paige! Open the door, it's just me. I got Chuck." She let out her breath and gave a shaky smile as she lowered the candlestick. She felt pretty silly jumping at every little sound. She put down the candlestick and buzzed off the alarm before opening the kitchen door.

Chuck burst through the door. His ears were sticking straight out, his eyes were bright with the excitement of the chase, and his tongue was flopping out the side of his mouth. He ran through the door and jumped up on her, his massive paws leaving mud stains on her shirt while he treated her to some of his slobbery kisses. He was quickly distracted by a bone in the living room and jumped down to trot out of the kitchen.

"What happened?" Paige asked as she opened her white wood cabinet and pulled out a glass. She turned on the tap and filled it with cold water for Cole. She took deep breaths to get her heart rate under control.

"Thank you." Cole smiled as he accepted the glass of water and took a long drink before answering. "I followed the sound of footsteps and almost caught up with him in the alley down by the feed store."

"Did you see him? Was it him?" Paige's hands started sweating again just thinking of the assassin nearby.

"No. I can't verify it for sure. He was in shadows, but it would make sense. Chuck almost got a bite into him, but he made it to his car with only a second to spare. That is one protective dog," Cole laughed. "You should have seen him. He went from this hodgepodge of ears and off-centered tail to a guard dog in a split second."

"Does this mean your undercover work is blown? You went after him. He'll know you're an agent now." Paige started to pace around her kitchen. If Cole's cover were blown, then it would put him in harm's way. The assassin wouldn't think twice about knocking off an FBI agent who was clearly after him.

"I got it covered, Paige. My cover wasn't blown. I didn't go after him. I went after Chuck since he was leaping into his car and about to burn rubber down the street. I wasn't close enough to get a shot off or to grab him, so I only called Chuck's name. Called him a bad dog and said he was making us late for dinner. When the guy jumped in the car, I yelled to him. I apologized for my dog scaring him as he drove away. I am pretty sure he heard me and I think I came off as the dutiful boyfriend chasing his girlfriend's dog as opposed to me chasing him."

Paige leaned against the island and felt her hands shaking. It had been a close call. What was worse was she had been scared out of her mind, pacing back and forth in the living room, when she realized she loved him. Paige groaned and buried her head in her hands. The man had run straight into danger for her. He was protecting her, even when she had fought so hard to hate him. Could karma kick her ass any harder?

"Paige, are you alright?" Cole asked, his voice dropping down to a husky whisper. She felt him step up next to her and place a hand on her shoulder. The heat traveled down her back and chased the fear away.

"Yeah, I am fine. I guess it's just the excitement of the night." She dropped her hands from her face and straightened up. Cole's hand slid up her neck, his fingers tracing her face. She looked up and into his face. His normally silver eyes were dilated black and left no question as to his desire.

He trailed his thumb over her bottom lip before bending down to capture her mouth with his. She sighed and felt the small moan escape her throat as she leaned into his embrace. His kiss was achingly slow and tender. She wanted more, though. They were not slow and tender. They were fire and ice. She ran her fingers through his black hair slowly and got the response she wanted. Cole growled and his tongue pressed into her mouth as he pushed her against the island.

Paige tightened her grip on Cole's hair and opened her mouth to him. She pressed against him, reveling in the feel of her soft body against his hard one. She couldn't seem to get close enough to him.

"Hmm. Paige, I am not doing this here." Cole groaned as he ripped his mouth from hers. His hand rested on her ass and he gave her cheek a squeeze before letting go.

Paige couldn't speak. Rejection stung and she pushed herself away from him. She couldn't believe it. It was happening all over again. Lead me on once, shame on him. Lead me on twice, shame on me, she thought.

"I am not doing this here. You deserve a bed and hours of attention, not a cold, hard counter. We can try that tomorrow, though." Cole gave her a bone-melting smile, scooped her up and carried her to the bedroom before she even had a chance to comprehend what was going on. When she did, she smiled and nuzzled into his chest, giving his earlobe a quick nip before Cole placed her gently onto her bed.

"I promise. I will do a very good job at protecting you from now on. I won't leave your side all night." He smirked as he tossed his shirt to the floor.

★　　★　　★

Paige felt her hand throbbing. She slowly cracked her eyes to the sun streaming into her room and found herself barely on the bed. Her arm was dangling off the side of the bed and her foot was so far over, her leg was almost touching the floor. She yawned and felt the tired muscles in her body from last night groan as she tried to wake them up. She turned her head on her pillow and looked into the face only a mother could love.

Chuck's massive chocolate head was on her pillow, his paws pushing into her side. She didn't know how she had managed to stay on the bed at all. Cole's arm was slung around Chuck's body as man and dog slept in noisy bliss as they tried to out-snore each other.

Paige slid the remaining inch out of bed and headed to the bathroom. She stretched and looked at herself in the mirror over the sink. The sunlight from the window filled the room with warmth. She decided great sex definitely did something for her complexion. She was practically glowing. She filled the sink with warm water to wash her face but froze when she heard a noise. She cocked her head and listened but didn't hear anything besides man and dog snoring in the bedroom.

She looked in the mirror and chided herself for allowing her imagination to run wild again. Last night obviously affected her more than she'd care to admit. She washed her face and patted it dry when she heard something again. Without putting down the hand towel, she crept toward the window that faced out back. She had half convinced herself it was nothing but a squirrel when she looked out and saw a man at the back door to her store.

The breath she was about to take froze in her lungs as she watched the man work her lock over. In slow motion, she watched as he raised his head and looked right at her. Their eyes locked and Paige felt the towel drop from her hands. She was staring into the cold brown eyes of the assassin.

Before Paige could scream, he reached into his jacket and pulled out a gun. He pointed it right at her and she finally forced herself to move. She leapt for the old iron bathtub as the first round was fired. She felt her naked body slam into the cold bathtub as the bathroom door was hurled open.

Cole was crouched with his gun drawn and scanning the room for her. She could tell the second he found her as he scanned her body for injuries and then headed straight for the window.

"Cole, be careful. It was him. He was at the back door of my shop trying to get in," Paige whispered as her fingers bit into the lip of the tub.

"He's not there now. Are you okay?" When she nodded, he held out his hand and helped her out of the tub. "I like your outfit. You look great this morning."

Paige looked down at herself and realized she was still naked. She looked over at Cole and took in his still-nude state. "You too," she said with a wink.

"While you get dressed I am going to call my boss. I want to see what's happening in New York and give him an update here." Cole walked to the bathroom window and looked at the small hole in the glass before closing the curtains. "Make sure to close all the curtains. He won't be able to get a clear shot that way." Cole walked over to her and grabbed her to him. He kissed her quickly and thoroughly before heading back into the bedroom to get his phone.

Paige closed the door and then sank onto the rim of the tub. Her legs had suddenly turned to jelly. Her heart was in her throat and there was no way she could possibly get dressed until she calmed down.

She put her head between her knees and took deep breaths to stop the dual feelings of nausea and passing out. When she finally felt like she could sit up again, she let out a long breath and sat upright. She looked in the mirror over the sink and felt dizzy all over again. Not only was she white as a ghost, she was still naked. "Oh God," she groaned as she turned the shower on. As if to add insult to injury, the assassin almost took her out while she was naked. She could just imagine Noodle and Dinky standing over her dead, naked body and the laugh Kandi would get out of it. Well, that settled that. She must try to remain clothed and looking fabulous at all times in case she was shot. She'd look good when Kandi came to finish her off with her claws.

By the time Paige had finished getting dressed, Cole strode into the bedroom with two coffee cups and a happy dog.

"I walked Chuck and he caught the man's scent right away. It looks like he parked down by the park and took off as soon as he fired at you."

"What did your boss say? How are things going in New York?"

"Ahmed and his group are already there. They are in meetings with the agents now. Everything is going well so far. They think they will have this wrapped up sometime this afternoon."

"So, what do we do in the meantime?"

"We open the shop and keep our eyes open for our assassin. They will give us a call when it's done and let us know what happened. And I will keep you as close to me as possible. He's getting bolder and it worries me. But if we want to catch him, we need to be patient and try to grab him the next time he shows up."

"This is torture. Not only do I have to keep my eyes open for the assassin and hope he makes another move to kill me, I also have to wait to see what happens in New York. Cole, I am not the most patient person." Paige drummed her fingers against the coffee mug and knew the day would go by excruciatingly slow. She would try not to look at the clock. She knew every peek would only result in five minutes ticking by. And she would try not to jump every time the door opened. She kept thinking she'd see him just walk through the door with his cold eyes. She shivered at the thought.

"Well, I can think of something we can do to kill some time." Paige looked up at Cole's wolfish smile and felt her shaky nerves start to shoot fire. All she could think of was feeling alive again. She had the added benefit that if it was anything like last night, maybe she could go a little longer than five minutes before she looked at the clock.

Chapter Nine

Contrary to what Paige had feared, the morning flew by. The whole town had heard of the shot fired at her this morning and had come out in force to hear the story straight from the source. John Wolfe had been the first person in her shop, followed quickly by Miss Edna. Miss Edna took it as a personal slight that John scooped her and had left as soon as Paige had told her what happened. According to the people who came into the shop after that, Miss Edna was taking a slight lead on the number of people she regaled with the story.

The bell tinkled again and Paige looked up from the gift she was wrapping for one of her customers. Paige couldn't keep the smile off her face if she tried. Mrs. Beauford Wyatt teetered in on her cane. Mrs. Wyatt had been in her eighties for as long as Paige had known her. The best way to describe Mrs. Wyatt was that she was born into the wrong century. She should have been parading around a veranda back before the Civil War. Similarly to those times, Paige didn't even know Mrs. Wyatt's first name. Once she married her husband, Beauford, she became Mrs. Beauford Wyatt.

She was dressed in a billowy white muslin dress. A special-order, large-brimmed black hat that Paige had made for her covered her white hair. Mrs. Wyatt never left the house without her "face on," as she called it. She powdered it with white powder and applied layers of bright red lipstick. Her cane was black with a silver horse head on top. Her cane was more for show than necessity. She liked to be able to give someone a good thwack if they got in her way or ticked her off.

"Paige! Bless your heart and twice for good measure. What is all this distressing news I have heard about you getting shot at?" Mrs. Wyatt shooed some of Paige's customers out of the way with her cane as she made her way, slowly and stately, to the counter.

"Mrs. Wyatt. It's so good of you to come all the way into town to check on me." Paige handed the gift-wrapped package to her customer and walked around the counter to kiss Mrs. Wyatt's wrinkled cheek.

"Nonsense. I had to check on the most famous and sought after hat maker according to the latest *Town & Country* magazine." Mrs. Wyatt reached into her enormous purse and pulled out a copy of the magazine.

A model with long black hair stood on the front cover in a tight black dress and a scarlet red hat that Paige had made for the Derby. Paige opened the magazine cover and flipped to the cover story about her hats. There was a picture of her shop and a picture of her at the Derby with Mo accompanying the story about how she makes her hats. Pride and quite a bit of astonishment filled Paige as she looked over the story on the up-and-coming hat maker from Kentucky.

"Thank you so much for bringing this in, Mrs. Wyatt! I had wanted to see it, but it's not on newsstands yet."

"I have a subscription, so I get it before the general public. As soon as I saw it, I knew I had to bring it down here." Mrs. Wyatt hefted her purse back onto her shoulder and fixed Paige with a hard stare. "Now, tell me what's going on young lady. Are you quite alright?"

"I am fine. Please don't worry. There have been some close calls. But with Chuck and Cole around, I am really quite safe."

"That's good to hear. I was so worried about you, my dear. Now that I know you are being well looked after, I can tell you my good news." Paige smiled as she waited for Mrs. Wyatt to continue. "My granddaughter, Katelyn, is arriving in two days!"

"That's wonderful news. I am sure you and Beauford will be thrilled to have her here. How long is she staying?"

"That's the best part. She's decided to open a veterinary clinic and is moving here permanently!"

"That is wonderful news. I look forward to getting to know her. Bring her by the shop once she gets settled. How did she decide to open her practice here?" Paige almost kicked herself for asking when she saw the smile on Mrs. Wyatt's face fade.

"Well, that no-good mother of hers, bless my daughter's heart, has run off with husband number seven to some country in Europe. When Katelyn graduated from Auburn Veterinary School, she had no home to go to. But maybe I can make up to Katelyn for whatever I did that turned Sylvia into such a weak-minded person when it comes to men."

"I am sure Katelyn will love being here with you and Beauford." Paige set the magazine on the counter and started to flip through it as Mrs. Wyatt started in on stories about Maggie, Floyd, Bart, and Fancy, who were some of her racehorses.

"Well, Fancy took to the starting gate faster than any… Damn!" Mrs. Wyatt stated as if it was part of the conversation. Paige looked up from the magazine and saw Kandi Chase-Rawlings strutting toward them with her husband, Bill Rawlings, meandering behind her.

"Oh, you poor dear!" exclaimed Kandi.

Paige raised an eyebrow at the strange, yet shrill comment. She had given up long ago trying to figure out what Kandi was talking about.

"It only took a couple of weeks to run this one off already."

Paige saw Kandi glance around the room as if making a point. Kandi turned and smirked at Bill, her domination complete over Paige. The bell over the door rang and the three white-haired Rose sisters walked in, clucking at each other in half sentences that only the triplets could understand. Paige smiled as they stopped in their tracks and stared at the sight of Kandi smirking. She saw them take in the black spandex miniskirt that barely covered her ass, the cropped ribbed tank top that left her belly exposed, and then to the massive dangling earrings that reminded Paige of Coke cans. She knew the sisters well enough to know they were salivating at the thought of watching another showdown between her and Kandi. Their showdowns were legendary in Keeneston.

"I head upstairs for just a moment to make you something to eat and the shop fills up. I guess I am no good for business," Cole chuckled as he walked down the stairs with a small tray in his hand.

Paige enjoyed seeing Kandi's smirk slide from her face and watched as Bill's normally self-assured confidence took a hit in reaction to seeing Cole walking down the stairs, dressed in a black t-shirt that fit tightly over his muscled chest and jeans, which were hanging low on his slim hips. Bill looked like a car salesman in a brown suit, orange shirt, and some kind of modern twist to a paisley tie. He also looked like an out-of-shape football player with his flabby belly and thinning hair. Ignoring Kandi and Bill, Cole walked past them, put the tray on the counter, and kissed her possessively on the lips.

"Missed you," he whispered as he placed a kiss on the soft skin under her ear. "Oh, hello, Cindy."

Paige heard the snickers and a snort that came from one of the Rose sisters who were now openly staring at the scene alongside Mrs. Wyatt. Kandi's face flushed red as she grabbed her husband's hand and stomped out of the shop.

"Hello, ladies." Paige hugged each of the sisters and felt a slight blush creep up her face when they all started talking about Cole at the same time.

"Bless your heart, whoever you are, that was the most entertainment I have seen in years. I can't wait to get home and tell Beauford about it." Mrs. Wyatt smiled at Cole and gently patted his arm.

"Mrs. Wyatt, this is Cole Parker, Cole, this is Mrs. Beauford Wyatt." Cole lifted Mrs. Wyatt's white-laced gloved hand and pressed his lips to it.

"A pleasure." Oh, he was good. Paige had never seen Mrs. Wyatt blush before and she was pretty sure the Rose sisters were about to swoon.

"Well, unless you're going to welcome all of us like that, let's get down to business." Miss Lily paused until she had everyone's attention. "We heard things were going down this afternoon in New York and we wanted to know how it went."

Paige couldn't decide if she should be surprised or not. As she stared at Cole's slightly opened mouth and momentarily stunned face, she decided it would be more unusual if they didn't know about it. She smiled; all was right with the world.

"Have you ever considered working for the Bureau? We need people with your sources on the ground overseas." Cole shook his head in disbelief. Before he could question the sweet, innocent-looking sisters, the bell over the door rang again as Red, Dinky, and Noodle sauntered in.

"Hey. How did the sweep go in New York?" Noodle asked with his slow and smooth Southern accent.

"Christ. Is there anyone who doesn't know about this?" Cole raked his hand through his raven hair. Paige just grinned. It felt safe, comfortable, to know the whole town knew about it and were just as concerned as she was.

The bell over the door rang again as Dani's parents entered with Mo's parents, along with Henry Rooney and John Wolfe. Dani and Mo's mothers clung to each other with nervous fear and the amusement Paige had been feeling vanished. This wasn't just about her. Dani and Mo's parents needed to know if the men who were behind Dani's attempted murder were caught.

"Take a deep breath, King, no news yet." Miss Violet patted Mo's father's arm and Paige worried for a second that she was going to pull him into her pillowed bosom to try to comfort him. He had deep worry lines around his mouth and on his forehead. Apparently the King had developed a soft spot for his soon-to-be daughter-in-law. Paige was glad for Dani. It had been a rough start between the two of them.

"If you have any nervous energy you need to work off, I can help with that." Henry slid up to her and placed an arm around her shoulder. His dentist-white smile sparkled and Paige felt herself relax. Henry had gone to school with Miles and Marshall. Even though they would beat the crap out of him if he ever touched her, he always did make her laugh.

She looked up when she heard a snarl and found Cole shooting silver daggers at Henry. Apparently Henry saw it, too, and pulled her closer, testing Cole's reaction. Before Paige could put an end to Henry's teasing, the bell rang again and Henry practically pushed her away from him as her brothers and parents walked in.

"Scaredy-cat," she whispered to him as he jumped away from her.

The room was pulsing with voices at various levels and tones. Paige leaned against the counter and took in the rhythm of the room. In the melody of conversation, a cell phone rang. She checked hers and saw many other people doing the same. As soon as the group figured out it was Cole's cell phone, a hush fell over the room. Her mother and father, trailed by her brothers, made their way to her side. She felt her mom's arm wrap around her waist and Miles's hand clasp her shoulder in silent support.

"Yes, sir. I will fill everyone in." Cole paused, "Um, yes, everyone as in the twenty people staring at me right now. Of course I didn't tell them. You have no idea the type of intelligence network they have in this town. Okay, I will see you Monday."

Cole hung up and Paige felt like she hadn't taken a breath in five minutes. He looked up from his phone and into forty anxious eyes. Paige squeezed Miles's hand and tried not to shout at Cole to hurry up with the news. Her stomach was in a tight knot and she couldn't tell if she wanted to sit down out of exhaustion or run ten miles because of the nervous energy coursing through her veins.

"Spit it out, young man. I think that traitor Sherman marched on Atlanta quicker than this," Mrs. Wyatt drawled. Cole smiled and then put on his cop face. Paige hated the cop face. Oh, this couldn't be good.

"There's good news and bad news. The bad news. They are not in jail right now." Paige felt like she was going to collapse. How could they not be in jail?

"The good news," Cole started, "is they found all the evidence they will need for a trial. They found the bodies of twenty-three girls out on Bob Greendale's property and found tire marks that match Senator Bruce's government-issued Suburban. As soon as the first body was found, my boss called the agents surrounding the houses and they moved in on the subjects. They were all taken to jail, fingerprinted, and had their passports confiscated. They are under house arrest until an indictment by the Special Grand Jury can be handed down on Monday."

He continued, "Ahmed apparently made sure to call the press a couple of minutes before he walked to the door of Bob Greendale's house. By the time the agents and Rahmi's Secret Service arrived at the police station, the media was a block thick. Due to the high profile of the case and the unimaginable details coming out, the press is eating this up. The mayor and governor are under considerable pressure for a quick trial and a harsh decision. As a result, my boss is faxing Red two grand jury subpoenas for Dani and Kenna. Kenna will be expected to fly to New York, Dani will give her testimony via video conference."

"I better get to the office and pick those up. I wager they need to be served immediately." Red said as he, Dinky, and Noodle said their goodbyes and headed for the station. Taking their cues, the shop began to empty and the crescendo of voices faded into the night.

"You okay?" Cole stopped in front of her and ignored her brother's protective glare.

"I guess. I was just hoping for something more definitive. Couldn't they arrest them, charge them, and try them all tonight? I would feel a lot better knowing they were in jail for the rest of their lives."

"Soon enough. With the media coverage and the political ramifications, the higher-ups will move this along quickly, regardless of the high-powered attorneys the defendants will hire.

There is something else. I need to go to New York and testify as well. Would you like to go with me to lend some support to Kenna? I know Will is going to go with her, but sometimes a friend is good to have there too."

"Yes, I would like to go with you. Anything to help Kenna." She felt Miles drop his hand from her shoulder as he pulled out his phone. He typed into the small keyboard and waited for a moment. His phone vibrated and he tucked it back into his pocket.

"It's all set," Miles said. "Cy will meet you there and help with security. When will you be arriving?"

"We need to be at the courthouse no later than eight in the morning. Ahmed is flying down with his security and some U.S. marshals in the private plane very early Monday morning. We will meet them at the Lexington airport at five in the morning. It will take two hours to fly there and the U.S. Assistant Attorney will be meeting us at the airport at seven to brief us on the way to the courthouse."

"I will send the information to Cy. He'll meet you at the airport." Miles punched some more buttons on his cell phone and then looked around at the family. With just a slight nod of their mother's head, each brother gave her a hug and a kiss goodbye and sent a pointed glare to Cole as they walked out.

"Take care, dear. We'll have dinner when you get back." Her mother placed a kiss on her cheek and followed her sons out the door.

"You be careful, sweet pea." Her father gave her a tight hug and then turned to Cole. "Anything happens to her and I will hold you responsible."

"Yes, sir." Cole shook her father's hand as they stared each other down. Her father grunted his approval and walked out the door.

★   ★   ★

Cole brought Chuck inside and double-checked the locks on the windows and doors before turning off the lights in the shop and heading up the stairs. Paige sat on her couch snacking on some food Miss Daisy and Miss Violet had brought over.

"You going to share?" Cole slid into the seat next to her and snagged a brownie.

"I wasn't going to, but you didn't really wait for an answer. I eat chocolate when I am nervous." She grabbed another brownie and wondered if Cole noticed she had already eaten a whole row of them. Maybe he would just think they had given her a partial tray of brownies?

"What are you nervous about?" Cole asked as he took a bite of the stolen brownie.

"Well, I know it's good news in New York. And I know those men will get what they deserve, but I am still worried about the assassin. Will he just give up now that his paycheck is in jail? I don't think so, and that is what is making me nervous." Crap, she looked down at her hand and saw nothing but crumbs. Okay, so it was a row and a half that had mysteriously disappeared.

She stared at the brownie tray and debated grabbing another one when she felt Cole's arm wrap around her shoulders and pull her against his chest. Oh, chocolate or sexy man who may or may not be her boyfriend? She stared longingly at the tray on the coffee table, but when his warm hand slid under her chin and brought her eyes up to his, all thoughts of chocolate vanished.

"I will always be here to protect you. You are the only thing that matters to me and I will do everything in my power to keep you safe," Cole whispered into her hair as he laid his cheek against her head.

Paige looked up into his eyes, dilated almost totally black, and found herself nervous for another reason. He leaned down and placed his lips on hers in a slow and achingly gentle kiss. Did he really care for her? Hope soared as she kissed him back with all the feelings raging inside her. She'd figure them out later. Right now she just wanted to feel.

"I bet I can take away your worries," He grinned down at her as he traced his thumb over her well-kissed lip. He slid his arm under her knees and pulled her down on the couch underneath him. That was a bet she was willing to take.

Chapter Ten

His phone rang as he paced the threadbare, olive-green carpet in his Lexington extended-stay hotel. He glanced over to the bed where he had tossed in frustration. He was supposed to be sitting on an island with scantily clad women walking by all day. Instead, he was stuck in a town with residents he deemed to be redneck intelligence officers.

Every time he tried to drive into town, he felt eyes on him as sweet little old ladies adjusted their glasses to see who the stranger was. Their knowing eyes made him so nervous that he usually turned around and went back to his hotel. There was only one person who knew what he looked like and that was the shop owner. He intended to take care of her tonight. He had been trying to limit the collateral damage, but not anymore. Even that ugly dog would get it if he interfered.

"Yeah," he answered the phone on the third ring.

"We have a problem."

"We sure do, judge." His idiot brother had gotten into trouble with the law. In return for hooking him up with the judge for this job, his brother's case had been dismissed on a technicality. But so far, this job had been one hassle after another. The first target was killed by the girl named Dani. Then the shop owner saw him. And now he kept getting calls from the judge.

"What do you mean, you have a problem? Haven't you taken care of the situation?"

"Not yet. I plan to tonight."

"Well, you better hurry. We're under house arrest and they are trying to get indictments on us on Monday. The majority of us could walk since there are no witnesses. We'd feel better if there were no loose ends to come back and bite us later."

"I'll take care of it." He hung up the phone and rubbed a hand over his eyes. It was time for retirement. His heart was no longer in it. He used to love his job. But now it was just one stress after another. He tossed the phone back on the bed and headed out the door for a jog before heading into Keeneston for the last time.

★   ★   ★

Paige stretched and opened her eyes slowly. Her room was awash in light. Since both Cole and Chuck were missing, she assumed they were out for a walk. She laid her head back down on the fluffy pillow and closed her eyes again. With the news of the New York bust hitting the streets of Keeneston Friday night, Paige's shop was crammed full of people on Saturday. She didn't have time to eat or even think about the amazing night she and Cole had shared. She had fallen into bed and slept like a log all night.

As she pulled her sheet up and snuggled in the bed, she couldn't help but smile. This fake relationship was now definitely a real one. Well, maybe. It had the appearance of being a real relationship, but they had not talked about what these nights together meant. She gave herself a mental headshake and decided to enjoy her time with Cole while it lasted.

"Morning," Cole whispered into her ear. "Or should I say afternoon."

"Afternoon!" Paige sat up and hit her head against Cole's strong jaw. "Ow." She rubbed her head and looked at Cole who was similarly rubbing his jaw. "Oops, sorry. I thought it was only ten."

"It was ten o'clock two hours ago. You were still asleep when I got back at eleven. I thought I would let you sleep since you've had a long couple of days."

Cole sat on the bed next to her and ran his hand over her hair and smirked. Paige lifted her hand and felt her hair standing at a strange angle and guessed she looked a lot like Chuck with his ears sticking straight out. She was surprised Cole wasn't running for the hills.

"Why don't you take a shower and get packed? I will make up some lunch and we can go to the park with Chuck." Cole stood up and Chuck instantly jumped off the bed to trail after him.

"Actually, I have a better idea. There is a place I would like to show you."

Two hours later she was clean, packed, and ready to go. She walked Chuck out to Cole's Explorer while he carried a picnic basket filled with fruit, sandwiches, and a second batch of brownies that Miss Violet delivered on her way home from church. They were going to have an early dinner at her favorite place before turning in early. Kenna was to be discharged from the hospital in the morning and they would meet her and Will at the airport at four-thirty. They were set to fly out at five. That meant she would be setting her alarm for three in the morning to give herself enough time to take a shower, eat breakfast, and drive to the airport in Lexington.

"So, where are you taking me?" Cole asked as he started the car.

"Head out of town on Main Street for about five miles." She clicked her seat belt and felt relaxed knowing she would soon be at her haven.

"Okay. So, you're not telling me where we are going?"

"Nope. It's a surprise." Paige smiled at him and was rewarded with one of his rare smiles that changed his whole face. Her heart leapt as she felt him place his hand on her knee and give it a squeeze.

"There are some things we should talk about before we leave tomorrow," Cole said seriously. "I want to talk about them now, lay out our plan, and then enjoy the rest of our day with no discussion about danger, law suits, or anything else related to this situation."

"Okay. What do we need to discuss?" Paige gripped her fingers together and hoped it wasn't anything bad. She was starting to become a big proponent of pretending the situation didn't exist, at least for a little while.

"First, I want to set up a designated safe spot. The courthouse is very close to Chinatown. If anything happens and I tell you to run, you run out of the courthouse and cut between the clerk's building and the district court. You will then be in Columbus Park. Run into the park and cut to your right. You will hit Mulberry Street. Take it away from the courthouse. Take the first right onto Mosco. It's a short street. When it ends, turn left onto Mott. Run to the intersection of Mott and Pell. You will be in the heart of Chinatown. There will be plenty of shops to duck into and hide until you see me standing on the corner. You think you can remember that?"

"Columbus Park, Mulberry, right Mosco, left Mott. Hide in shops at Mott and Pell until you come for me. Got it. Anything else?"

"Yes. I am going to have to leave you for a bit. I have to give testimony to the grand jury. While I am doing that, you will be locked in a room with Kenna, Will, a slew of U.S. marshals, and Ahmed."

"Don't forget Cy."

"I don't know if Cy can get clearance, but I will try."

"It's already done. Miles got it yesterday morning. Cy will be cleared to go anywhere with me," she stated matter-of-factly.

"What exactly does Cy do?"

"I don't know. Technically, he's a farmer, but he disappears multiple times a year for weeks at a time. Sometimes he comes back with a broken bone or some bruises. So far, the family money is on UFC-type fighting. Whatever it is, it takes him all over the world."

"You've never asked him?"

"Of course we have. He just says he doesn't want to say and gets really defensive about it. I think he's embarrassed about whatever it is." She pointed to a small dirt road a mile past her parents' driveway. "Oh, turn right here."

Cole turned down the drive and bounced along the rutted road for what seemed like forever. They passed cows and corn and finally came to the open field that was the entrance to the creek.

"Okay. Stop here," she told Cole.

"This is the place?" he asked with trepidation.

"No. This is where we all used to play football and soccer. We're going through the woods there," she pointed to a path that went into the woods across the field.

Chuck barked excitedly and clawed at the window to get out and run. She hopped out of the truck and opened the door for him. He bounced around for a minute before his nose shot up in the air. He took a sniff of the wind and then took off for the woods.

"I assume it's okay for him to run off like that?" Cole asked as he picked up the picnic basket to follow her toward the path.

"Yes. All of this is my parents' property. And, my parents' property is surrounded by my brothers' property. So there's no place for him to really go. He just likes to run in the woods and pretend he's a mighty hunter."

Paige started to walk down the path in the woods and instantly felt relief. The shade from the trees in the woods made the hot summer day bearable as she soaked in the smells of the trees and grass and the sounds of the breeze rustling the leaves. Rays of sunlight twinkled through the thick green leaves and danced around them as the leaves moved in the breeze.

"We head down here about a half-mile and then we hit Bear Creek. That's my special place. No matter how stressed I am, or how upset I am, I can always come here and the tension just falls away. I think it's the quiet and the smell of the country. Then there's also the relaxing bubbling of the creek and the cool water to hang your toes in." She looked up when she heard the crashing sounds of Chuck running through the brush and laughed as he happily leapt onto the path ahead of them with his tongue hanging out the side of his mouth.

"It is nice here. I can't believe it's so much cooler than in town."

Cole looked good out here, she thought. His sunglasses were pushed up on his head. His shirt pressed against his hard chest and abs as he walked. And he had a relaxed smile on his face.

"It's my favorite place in the whole world." She took the last couple of steps to the top of a small mound and looked down to her paradise.

Three large stones sat partially obscuring the wide creek. The first two, each around four feet, lay on the bottom. The third one, about five feet in diameter, sat on top of the other two rocks. Most of the lower stones were underwater, creating a small, one-foot waterfall between the two stones.

She turned her head and looked up the creek. It was like a liquid roadway flowing between a tunnel of trees. The water level was higher due to the backup caused by the rocks. In the summer, she'd strip down and go swimming. If there was enough rain, it could be as deep as four feet. Downstream from the rocks, the water was usually around two feet and flowed much quicker.

"This is great." Cole set the basket down and put his arm around her waist, pulling her in close for a quick kiss on the head. "Thanks for sharing this with me. But how do we get down there?"

"How's your balance, Parker?" She pointed to an old fallen tree that landed on the far side of the creek. You could walk down and then jump off the left side to land on the far side of the middle rock.

"Not that great."

"Don't worry, I'll show you a trick." She picked up the basket and stepped toward the creek bank. There were five walking sticks leaning against a nearby tree. She grabbed one and put it down into the creek. She grasped the top of the stick and used it to help balance her as she quickly walked down the fallen tree. She picked up the stick, turned, and jumped the short distance to the rocks before flashing a smile at Cole. She moved to the other side of the rock and set the basket down.

"Your turn." She grinned as Cole nervously placed his first foot on the tree. She had left the tallest stick for him to use, but he was still wobbling quite a bit. He inched his way down the tree and leapt as soon as he could onto the rock.

"Well, that wasn't too bad." Cole placed his walking stick next to hers and joined her on the edge of the rock. "This is really cool. I love this little waterfall."

They both turned upstream when they heard the loud splash. Cole laughed as he watched Chuck lazily swim around before reaching the rocks.

"Duck and cover!" Paige yelled as she turned to protect the picnic basket. It started with a little shake of Chuck's nose and turned into a downpour as Chuck shook all the way to the tip of his tail. He sent water flying and somehow it all landed on Cole.

Paige couldn't stop laughing. Chuck sat there with his tongue drooping out of his mouth while his tail thumped the rock making Cole dripping wet.

"Oh, you think this is funny, do you?" Cole lunged for her and wrapped her in a big hug, getting her just as wet as he was. She tossed her head back and laughed louder and Chuck started dancing around them barking.

Paige cleared the plates and tossed the extra food into the woods for the animals. Chuck was off hunting on the far side of the creek and Cole lounged back on his elbows. She untied her shoes and peeled off her socks and stood up.

"Come on. Take off your shoes and socks. I was smart and wore shorts, but you can just roll your jeans up." She placed her hands on her hips and waited for him to comply.

"Why am I doing this?" Cole asked as he took off his running shoes.

"We're going creeking," she smiled.

"Creeking?"

"Yup. It's when we go for a walk in the creek. It's very pretty downstream, especially down around the bend. There's a place where the silt is replaced by small rocks and creates a beautiful ripple effect as the water flows over it."

She slid off the rocks and into the cool water. It refreshed her instantly as she wiggled her toes in the soft creek bottom. Cole made a rookie mistake as he jumped in from the rocks instead of sliding in.

"Holy shit! I am stuck." He looked at her with pleading eyes. She walked over to him and held out her hand.

"Here. Take my hand. Now, move your leg to the left and then the right. Just wiggle it out. This is a silt-bottom creek. It's really easy to get stuck. If you do, you just wiggle your foot until it pops out." With a sucking noise, the creek gave up and let go of Cole's foot.

In less than a minute he was free and getting the feel of walking the creek. He caught up to her and slipped his hand into hers. When she looked up at him, he smiled down at her and let her lead him down the creek.

"Thank you for such a great afternoon and evening," Paige said as she snapped her seat belt on as Cole loaded a worn-out Chuck into the back seat.

"No. Thank you. That sunset was beautiful and dinner on the rocks was amazing." Cole climbed into the seat and gave her a bone-melting smile.

His smile dimmed as he looked at her lips. He cupped her chin with his hand and tilted it up toward his lips. He leaned down and kissed her with a slow, burning passion. Paige flung her arms around his neck, which threw fuel on the fire. He pulled her over the console and into his lap. His hands found their way under her shirt and cupped her breasts. Paige moaned and pulled back.

"How fast do you think you can get us home?"

Cole helped her back into the seat and winked at her challenge. Dirt flew as he tore out of the field.

Cole brought his mouth to hers the second she got out of the car. He dragged her against him as they stumbled through the front door. As soon as the door was closed and locked, he tugged her shirt over her head as they made their way to the stairs.

By the time they were halfway up the stairs, she had his shirt off and they had both kicked off their shoes and socks. As they entered her living room, her bra was somewhere on the stairs, next to her panties and his boxer briefs. They had managed to unclothe while touching constantly. His lips were on hers or placing kisses down her neck. She moaned as he rolled her nipple between his fingers. Fireworks exploded and suddenly he was pushing her to the ground.

"Keep down!" Cole covered her body with his as glass shattered and gunfire erupted. He leaned over and grabbed the heavy iron table and slid it to them. He pushed it over, causing her beautiful glass vase to shatter as it fell to the ground. She heard Chuck barking madly over the sound of gunfire from the kitchen.

"Chuck!" She tried to yell but found her screams muffled in Cole's bare chest. She felt him whistle and then lunged quickly off her, grabbing Chuck's collar and hauling him down behind the table. She didn't know how long it lasted, but when silence fell it was deafening.

"Stay down," Cole ordered as he poked his head up and over the table. When no one tried to shoot him, he opened the door to the shop and darted through the door. Seconds later, he was back with his jeans and shoes on, carrying his gun.

Tears streamed down Paige's face as she thought about all she had lost. If they had shot into the downstairs as well, her shop would be destroyed, just like her house. Cole didn't need to tell her to stay down. She had a death grip on Chuck and tried to prepare herself for what she was going to see. From what she could see, her wall was Swiss cheese.

"Well, that killed the mood." Cole tried to get her to smile as he came out of the hallway with a pair of jeans, some sneakers, and a t-shirt from her bedroom. "You may want to hurry. You know everyone will be here soon. This wasn't covert. This was an all-out attack."

"My shop?" She strangled out between the silent sobs racking her body.

"It's okay, sweetheart. He only hit your apartment." Cole pulled her in for a hug, but he pushed her back too soon. "Fire and police are already here. I would really like it if no one else saw you naked. I will carry Chuck downstairs so he doesn't step on any glass. I will hold them off for a minute, but they'll need to get in here soon." He kissed her on the forehead and picked Chuck up.

Hmm, no underwear. She slid on her jeans and her shirt without really sitting up. She turned her back to the apartment and laced up her tennis shoes. She stood and took a deep breath before turning around. Tears sprang to her eyes and the breath was knocked out of her. Her apartment was ruined. Her walls were filled with bullets. Anything with glass was shattered. She slowly looked around at her damaged kitchen. When she turned back to the living room, she almost fainted. The table they were hiding behind was completely shot up. The thick slate had prevented them from being killed.

Paige walked down the stairs on wobbly legs. The team of firefighters and deputies made their way past her and into what was left of her apartment. She breathed a sigh of relief when she saw that her shop was not damaged, but it was short-lived. The front door was already open and the Rose sisters poured in along with Marshall. At the sight of her brother, she broke into a new set of tears.

"It's okay, Sis." He wrapped his large arms around her and she gave into the loud body-wracking tears she had been trying so hard to hold back. When she looked up, she saw that Cole was gone and that the Rose sisters were already on the phone by the cash register. The church phone tree had been activated.

"Can Chuck stay with you tonight?" she choked out in between sobs.

"Of course. You know Bob will like the company." Bob was Marshall's dog and the smartest dog she'd ever met.

"Come on, sweetheart, let's get you to your parents' house. We'll spend what's left of the night there. I have a feeling your parents will feel better if they can see you." Paige brought her tear-streaked face up from Marshall's shoulder and looked into Cole's worried eyes.

"I thought you were supposed to keep my sister safe! Don't think I don't know what was going on. My sister has no bra on, you have no shirt on, and there is a pair of boxers and a bra lying on the stairs. You're supposed to be protecting her, not sleeping with her!" Marshall glared at Cole.

"Marshall! It's none of your business who I sleep with. Besides, he saved me. Go upstairs. He protected Chuck and me with his own body and he pulled the table down in front of us. Go upstairs, Marshall, and look at that table. Then come down here and apologize." Paige's tears dried up as anger took over. Cole had saved her life and had even risked his own life to protect her dog. There was no way she'd ever forget that.

She watched Marshall send one last glare to Cole and head upstairs. "Paige." It was a plea that she answered to the delight of the Rose sisters looking on. She flung herself into his arms and kissed him with all she had.

"Thank you."

"I don't know what I would have done if I lost you." He kissed her again before they heard Marshall clear his throat.

"I do owe you an apology. Take her to my parents and keep her safe." Marshall shook Cole's hand and watched them make their way down the stairs. "And Parker, put on a shirt for crying out loud." He flashed a quick grin before heading back upstairs.

Cole pulled into the driveway leading to her parents' house. They hadn't said anything on the drive over. Cole had just put their luggage in the car, kissed her, and driven off. She wanted nothing more than to hug her family and go to bed.

The house came into view and was lit up bright as day. Her parents stood arm-in-arm on the patio along with Miles, Cade, and Pierce.

"Good think I put on my shirt," Cole quipped. Paige laughed and felt some of the fear disappear.

Her mother flew down the patio and opened her door as soon as Cole stopped the car. Paige lost herself in the feel of her mom's comforting embrace while her father made his way down the stairs.

"Marshall called us and told us what happened. It seems I owe you for my daughter's life." Her father shook Cole's hand and led him into the house.

"Come on, dear. Let's get you tucked in."

Paige followed her mother and felt the tension in the room escalate again. She turned around to see Cole following her. Miles stepped forward and put a hand on his shoulder.

"That's not all Marshall told us when he called." He looked pointedly at Cole and then at the couch in the living room. "I'll go get you a pillow."

Chapter Eleven

Mo's private plane started its descent over New York City. Kenna and Will were still asleep in the bedroom. Cole was on the phone organizing security. Paige had gotten a text message from Cy saying he was already at the airport with the attorney and a bunch of marshals.

"Can you go wake up Kenna and Will and tell them they have fifteen minutes?" Cole asked as he covered the phone with his hand.

"Sure." She tore her eyes away from the sun rising over the skyline and headed to the back of the plane.

Will answered the door after she knocked and she found that they were already dressed. "We'll be out in just a minute. It's really good you're here, Paige." He kissed her cheek quickly before closing the door.

"Sweetheart, can I have minute?" Cole hung up his phone and patted the seat next to him on the couch.

"Sure, what is it?"

"Let me know if anything feels off. If you have bad vibes from anyone, then let me know. If I am not around, shut off the GPS on your phone, take your brother, and disappear in Chinatown. Okay?"

"Do you really think something will happen?"

"No. But I want plans in place just in case something does go wrong." Cole pulled her onto his lap and kissed her. "Just be careful. I will hate not being by your side all day."

"Don't worry about me. Focus on your testimony. I will be with lots of marshals and Cy."

"Yeah, I don't know how much trust I put into a farmer."

"Did I mention Cy's the black sheep of the family?"

"What does that mean? He has blue eyes?" he laughed.

"Let's it put it this way; he makes Miles seem like a compliant kitten." She laughed at Cole's expression and kissed him as the plane landed on the private runway.

"So, are we going to do this thing or what?" Kenna walked out of the bedroom dressed in her best courtroom attire: tailored black suit, white silk shell, and black pumps. Her auburn hair was tied up in a French twist and her black sling was hardly noticeable against the dark suit.

"Let's do this." Cole stood up and slipped on his suit coat. Ahmed approached from the cockpit and opened the door.

"Here's how it's going to work. I will go out first. I will talk with the people on the ground and make sure everything checks out. Only then will I come back and get you. If I am not back in five minutes, then the pilot will take off. I will stick with Kenna all day as Miles has sworn Cy will be able to stick with Paige. Everyone clear?" When he heard the chorus of agreements, he pushed the door back and headed down the stairs.

"Okay, we're clear." Three minutes later Ahmed led Will and Kenna down the stairs. Cole slipped Paige's hand in his and smiled down at her as they made their way down the stairs. Cole jerked to a halt at the bottom of the stairs.

"Crap. He is scary." Paige followed Cole's eyes and smiled when she saw her brother. Though he was the same height as Cole, Cy had at least thirty pounds of muscle on him. What made him scary was the way his hazel eyes could bore through a person. Paige dropped Cole's hand and ran to her brother.

"Cy!" She leapt into his open arms and he spun her around.

"Hey, Sis."

"It's so good to see you again. It's been months!" She hugged him tight and squeezed with all her might. Cy was just two years older than she was, making him the closest brother in age.

"It seems a lot has happened in the months I have been away. I guess I will need to come home more often." He was shooting icicles at Cole as he walked forward. She had to give Cole points. He kept his strides even and maintained eye contact with Cy the whole way.

"Special Agent Cole Parker."

"Cy Davies."

Paige rolled her eyes as the men stared each other down.

"My brothers have told me all about you." It sounded more like a threat, but Paige was surprised when Cole just smiled.

"Good. Then I can do this and not have to answer any questions." He turned to her and gave her a quick possessive kiss. "I have to go meet with the attorney. Then we'll be ready to head out." He gave her another quick kiss on the lips before heading over to the lovely young attorney who was clearly unable to keep her eyes off Cy.

"Okay, Sis, I like him." Cy smiled and rocked back on his heels. "He's the only boyfriend with enough balls to talk to me."

Men, Paige thought as she rolled her eyes and slipped her hand into the crook of his arm.

The three black Suburbans pulled to a stop at the side entrance of the federal courthouse. Three U.S. marshals cleared the way while Cy and Cole sandwiched Paige. Ahmed and Will surrounded Kenna. As soon as they cleared security, Paige slipped her hand into Kenna's for support.

McKenna Mason had practiced in this courthouse before. She had told Paige the last time she stepped foot in here she had won a case. It had to be good luck. Paige looked at her and took in her exterior. Her face was relaxed and confident. Her stride was strong and sure. Her hair and dress remained perfect. But Paige felt the tremors in her hand. She gave Kenna a gentle squeeze.

"You'll do great. You're the best attorney I have ever met and the best one to ever practice in Keeneston!" She was rewarded by a quick laugh and a return squeeze of the hand.

"Thanks. I am so glad you're here. Cole is testifying first, then me. After I get it over with, I will have to thank your brother, too." Kenna glanced over her shoulder and took a quick look at Cy. "He is rather scary-looking."

"It's the cold stare. He's actually sweet as can be." Paige laughed when Kenna snorted.

They followed Ahmed into a private conference room on the fourth floor. "This isn't the right floor. The courtroom is on the fifth floor."

"For security we wanted you close but not obvious. You would normally be in the conference room directly above us. Just in case anyone got any ideas, we wanted you hidden. One of the marshals will be in the courtroom to signal us when you are needed. At that time, we will bring you upstairs," Ahmed told her. "Your attorney is downstairs talking with the judge. Cole will be going first." He turned to Cole. "You'll head down there in fifteen minutes."

Kenna and Will took a seat at the far side of the room near the back door. Four marshals, Cy, Cole, Paige, and finally Ahmed filed into the room. The marshals stood by the doors and Paige took a seat next to Cole to start the process of waiting.

Paige was worried sick the whole time Cole was gone. He'd been gone for three hours and she was running out of stories to tell Kenna. Her goal had been to take her mind off the testimony and to make her laugh if possible. Ahmed pulled out his phone and looked at it the same time the marshals did. The room held its breath waiting to hear the news.

"Cole has finished. He's on his way down now. Kenna, it's time for us to take you up." Ahmed stood up, as did the four marshals. Kenna took a deep breath and looked around the room.

"Thanks, Paige. I would be tearing out my hair if you hadn't been here." She kissed Will and followed Ahmed out the door.

"I can't thank you enough." Will wrapped Paige up in a hug. "I kept on trying to think of things to say. But there was no way I could have talked for three hours like you did. You kept her relaxed and you kept me relaxed. Now, do you think you can talk for another three hours to keep me sane?" Will laughed.

"I'll try." She turned when the door opened and rushed to Cole and gave him a hug. "How did it go?"

"It was fine. Just answered lots of questions." Cole turned to Will and slapped him on his back. "Kenna will do great. She may not have to be up there as long as I was."

A knock on the door sounded. Cole and Cy shoved Paige behind them. There was silence in the room until another knock sounded.

"Parker, you in there?" Paige felt Cole let out a breath and smiled as he unlocked the door.

A man in his late fifties with gray hair in the classic side-part cut and generic black suit walked into the room. He and Cole shook hands.

"Damn good to see you again, Parker."

"You too, sir." Cole pumped the older man's hand and grinned.

"How did it go in there?"

"Really well, sir."

"Good to hear. I am heading in there after that pretty young lady gets done."

"Ah, well that pretty young lady is McKenna Mason," Cole gestured to Will, "and this is her husband, Will Ashton. Will, this is my contact in D.C., Director Phillip Salmond. And this is Paige Davies."

Paige smiled and shook the man's hand. She couldn't help feeling slighted, though. Cole used no identifier when he introduced her. She couldn't help feeling slightly insecure about where their relationship stood.

"Nice to meet you, ma'am. I hear you're having a tough time yourself. How are you doing?"

"I am managing. Thank you. I luckily have a lot of family and town support."

"Yes, your family is pretty remarkable. I almost feel sorry for the guy not knowing what he was getting into. I bet you don't scare easily being raised with all those boys. And as for your town, I am fascinated. How did they learn about the New York operation?"

Before Paige could answer, Phillip's phone beeped. He pulled it out of the inside pocket of his suit and read the message.

"They have about thirty more minutes with Ms. Mason. I am being called up to review some documents before I go on the stand. Before I go, I have to tell you, Mr. Ashton, that I am a big fan. I tried to make it to every game when you were playing in D.C. Well, it was nice to meet you all and I am sure I'll see you at the trial." He shook hands again with Parker. "Let me know if you need any additional resources to look after Miss Davies here. I'll be more than happy to send them to you."

"Thank you, sir. I will keep you updated."

Paige paced the small room and kept her eye on the clock hanging on the back wall. It had been thirty-five minutes since Agent Salmond left. The whole room was anxiously awaiting Kenna's return. Cole talked to Will about football to distract him from the fact that time had ground to a halt. After what seemed like an eternity, which was really only three more minutes, the door unlocked and Kenna walked through.

Her face was still masked in lawyer mode, but her nails were no longer digging into her palms. Will rushed to her and wrapped her up in a hug.

"Are you okay?"

"Yes, I am fine. I am glad to have it done. It seemed like they were more interested in the technical stuff from Cole than my testimony. But it really took a lot out of me. Not counting having the pregnancy sleepiness. Are we staying here or going home tonight? Either way, I just want a bed."

Paige saw Ahmed step out into the hall as she gave Kenna a hug. "Are they going to have to call Dani?" she asked Kenna.

"No, I don't think so. The case seems pretty iron-clad. I think the defendants will just start turning on each other. Bob and Senator Bruce are going to come out with the worst of it. That is, unless Cole can catch the assassin and find out who hired him. I think the vice mayor is an idiot, and he'll probably be the first to turn for a reduced sentence. Especially since I don't think he's smart enough to plan any of this."

"The plane is being fueled right now and will be ready to depart in fifteen minutes. The marshals are bringing the cars around now. We'll be in Keeneston in time for dinner," Ahmed said as he walked back into the room.

"Good, let's go home." Will slid his arm around Kenna and tucked her under his shoulder as they headed out the door.

Chapter Twelve

Paige was exhausted. After arriving in Lexington, they had driven to Marshall's house to pick up Chuck. Now they were finally headed back to her apartment to pick up some clothes to take to her parents' house. She had gotten only a couple hours of restless sleep last night and, even though it was only seven at night, she was ready for some food, then bed.

Cole pulled the Explorer into the back parking lot and opened the door for her. She leaned on him as they gave Chuck a quick walk and then headed up the back staircase. Paige had already dug her key out and had to blink a couple of times to get the lock to stop moving around. She pushed open the door and gasped.

"What is it?" Cole shoved his way past her and froze. The kitchen was clean. It was spotless. She figured on the new door and windows, but there were new plates, artwork, table, and chairs.

Paige was speechless. She walked through the kitchen with her hand skimming the new countertops and entered the living room. Her mom had obviously been part of the fairy godmothers who swooped in and fixed up the place. Now she knew what the phone tree was about the other night. It wasn't for the typical food but to help fix her place. There were pictures from her mother's living room hanging on the walls and a couple of her grandmother's blankets lying across a new couch.

"This is amazing." Cole turned round and round checking out the handiwork.

Paige made her way down the hall and toward her bedroom filled with the love that came from having a great family and caring friends. As she walked toward her bedroom, all thoughts of the day left and were replaced with a deep desire for her bed and the sleep that would soon follow. She hadn't been in her bedroom since the shootout and didn't know what to expect. She pushed open the door and screamed.

A man in khaki pants, white dress shirt, and black ski mask stood in the center of her room with a gun leveled at her. She heard Cole yell her name but couldn't make out what he was saying. She was caught in the cold stare that dug into her from behind the ski mask. That stare held her rooted in place. She would recognize those dead brown eyes anywhere.

"Please don't shoot up my apartment again," Paige squeaked out. All she could think about was all the work people did to fix her apartment and hoped it wasn't ruined again.

"There is no 'again'. This is the last time we'll meet." He pulled the hammer back and Paige knew this was it. She prayed the Hail Mary and closed her eyes. Her mind flashed to her family and then to Cole. She was overtaken with the sadness of knowing she would never see them again. The sadness was so heavy it prevented her from breathing.

Suddenly her breath was taken from her as she was knocked off her feet by a seventy-five-pound freight train rushing past her. A dark blur of fur and teeth flew past her and Chuck growled in a way she had never heard. It was so deep and vicious the hair on her arms stood up as she watched the dog leap into the air in front of her. Chuck landed a vicious bite on the assassin's arm. Paige's view of Chuck was blocked when a shot rang out. She heard glass shattering and then nothing more as Cole tackled her to the ground while reaching for his gun.

Cole pinned her to the ground with his body, preventing her from seeing what was going on. Even though blood was racing through her head, she could tell there was silence. Cole jumped off her and ran to the window, looking out the back.

"Dammit!" Cole shouted as he looked out the broken window. He leveled his gun and fired off a couple of rounds and then turned. "He got away. Good news, he's bleeding. Bad news, your azalea bush is squashed from where he jumped out the window."

Paige couldn't pay attention to what Cole was saying as tears filled her eyes. Chuck wasn't moving. She crawled toward his still body, fearful of what she would find as Cole kept talking and making phone calls.

"Chuck. Chuck! Can you hear me, buddy?" she cried as she got closer. Tears blinded her as she reached him.

"Oh no, Paige. Is he shot?" Cole was by her side and she grabbed onto his shirt as she shook with tears.

"I don't know. He's not moving and when I called him he didn't respond." Paige placed her hand on his face and stroked his face. "Chuck? Come on, sweetie, please be okay." She felt the weight of the situation settle on her as she buried her face in his neck and cried for her best friend.

"I am so sorry, sweetheart. He saved your life and I will never be able to thank him for it. Why don't you sit down here on the bed and I will take care of him for you." Cole helped her to the bed and then went back to Chuck. "You were a good boy, my friend." He ran a hand down Chuck's head before bending down and sliding an arm under Chuck's neck. He slid his other arm under his back legs. As he went to pick him up, Paige heard the unmistakable sound of a whine.

"Cole?" Paige's breath caught in her throat. The tears streaming down her face slowed and she strained to see if she had just imagined the sound.

"Chuck?" He ran his hands over her dog and turned to her with a smile. "There's no blood!"

Paige dropped to the floor next to them and placed her ear to Chuck's chest. "There's a heartbeat!" She had never known such relief in all her life. New tears started flowing down her face as she covered Chuck's body with hers and whispered what a good boy he was to him.

"Chuck was probably knocked unconscious by the gunman when he attacked." Cole leaned down and yelled, "Hey!" into Chuck's ear and was rewarded with a small lick. "Thank God!" Cole caught Paige as she flung herself at him, tears of joy rolling down her face.

Chuck's eyes fluttered open and he whined again before mustering up a single tail thump. Paige gently petted his head and told him what a hero he was.

"Paige, it may be time to put you in a safe house." She didn't want to admit he was right. She was petrified. All she could see when she closed her eyes was the barrel of the gun and those cold eyes. But right now she was tired, so very tired.

"Let's talk about it tomorrow. I can't think straight right now."

"Okay. Go get ready for bed and I will get Chuck up onto the bed." Paige gave Chuck another kiss before grabbing a nightshirt and heading into the bathroom to brush her teeth.

Chuck was tucked into bed with his tail wagging under the covers and Cole was taping a garbage bag over the broken window. Paige pulled down the covers to what was quickly becoming her side of the bed and climbed in. She tried to stay awake to talk to Cole, but she succumbed to the exhaustion before he could even finish taping up the window.

With the weekend events, the trip to New York, and the latest shootout at her apartment, the shop was packed all day long. Things were flying off the shelves as the whole town turned out to hear the news. The Rose sisters practically ran the cafe out of her store so they wouldn't miss anything.

"Oh, you poor thing!"

Paige groaned at Kandi's grating snobby voice. "You must be going out of business. Why, your shelves are bare! And here I was going to see if you were going to participate in the Summer Festival at the end of the month. Oh, that is just too bad. You know, if you need to sell the place, I was thinking of dabbling in a little store like this for fun."

"I am not going out of business. Actually, the shelves are bare because I have sold out of most my things and haven't had time to restock the shelves with new items. Of course, I will set up a table for the Summer Festival. Go ahead and sign me up. Thanks for thinking of me." Paige was too tired and busy to fight with Kandi.

"Great," Kandi said, but it came out shrill. "I'll put you down on the list. You know, Bill and I are thinking of going away on a little romantic vacation. We were thinking a quick trip to the Keys. You have anything sexy I could surprise him with?" Paige tried not to roll her eyes. Kandi was under the misunderstanding that Paige still cared for Bill. While he might have hurt her and caused her to have a jaded relationship history, it did not mean she was holding a candle for him.

"Sorry, Kandi. I only have things for teenagers and younger, nothing appropriate for our age." Paige didn't mean for it to sound snide, but apparently Kandi thought differently and flounced out of the store in a huff. Would she ever be able to just have a civil conversation with Kandi? After everything she had gone through these past couple of months, dealing with a person still holding onto high school differences just didn't seem worth it.

Cole closed the door after shooing the last customer out the door as politely as he could. He locked the door and turned back to her. "Wow, what a day!"

"I know. Getting shot at is good for business. No wonder rappers do it."

"Well, come on upstairs while I walk Chuck. You can check out your new window, um, again." Cole clipped the leash onto the fully recovered Chuck and headed out the back door.

Her feet throbbed from the busy day as she walked upstairs. She pushed opened the door into her private rooms and inhaled the smell of garlic bread. She kicked off her shoes and squished her toes in the new rug before heading to the kitchen. Her small table was set with two plates and a candle was lit at the center of the table. Warm garlic bread sat on the island along with a salad and another large bowl. She lifted the towel covering it and saw chicken Alfredo with mushrooms and broccoli.

"I thought I would make you dinner after such a long day," Cole said as he and Chuck entered the room.

"Thank you. This is beautiful and smells delicious." Cole smiled and held out the chair for her. "Not as beautiful as you and not nearly as nice as you deserve."

★　　★　　★

Dammit! How had things turned out this way? It was all because of his idiotic brother. He should have just retired and left his brother to rot in jail. Now his reputation was in tatters and that bitch was still alive thanks to her ugly dog. Where in the hell had he come from? He hadn't even seen him and then the dog had suddenly attacked. He rubbed his bandaged arm and grimaced at the pain. He stopped his mental rant when the phone rang. He crossed the room to pick it up.

"Yeah."

"We need you to lay low for a while. You think you can hang out there for a week or two and then quietly finish the job?"

"Sure. What's with the wait?"

"It doesn't look good with the indictment and I don't want anything to happen right now that would jeopardize us not being able to get house arrest until our trial. We need to regroup and plan our next step. Just give it some time and then make it look like an accident. Murder-suicide after evidence of an affair is discovered. Or maybe a car accident... something like that."

The phone clicked off and he threw the phone onto the bed. Sure, he'd give it some time. But after shooting up her place twice, he didn't think any kind of accident would be believable. However, regrouping sounded like a good idea. He'd follow her. Lead her into a false sense of security and then strike. She'd never see it coming.

★　　★　　★

A ringing phone penetrated her sleepy haze. Paige heard Cole answer it as she forced her eyes open. She looked over at the clock and mumbled incoherently when she found it was only seven o'clock. She had slept almost twelve hours.

"Good news and bad news," Cole said as he sat down on the new yellow down comforter.

"Okay. I am up. Tell me." She sat up in bed and waited for Cole to tell her the news.

"Everyone was indicted. Ranging from twenty-three counts of murder for Bob and Bruce down to accessory to murder for the rest of them. The trial has been set for next month."

"Good. What's the bad news?"

"Because of their status in the community, they were given house arrest. I don't doubt for one moment they are in constant contact with each other planning their next step. I would place money on this not making it to trial because of them disappearing."

"Really?"

"Yeah, but I will talk with Salmond and see what we can do to make sure they stay put. In the meantime, I have a surprise for you. Come on, throw these jeans on. I have an idea of how to celebrate the indictment and let you blow off some steam, too." Cole flashed her a smile right before tossing the jeans to her.

★　　★　　★

Paige jumped from the Explorer and took in the smell of oats, manure, and hay. It was the best smell in the world. It was only eight in the morning, but Keeneland race track was alive with activity. She looked down the rows of barns where grooms where bathing horses and trainers were walking horses to and from the track.

"This is great, Cole. I used to ride all the time. I even worked here one summer in high school as a groom." Paige took another deep breath and let the smells fill her lungs.

"I know. That's why I thought you would enjoy an hour of riding." Cole rocked back on his heels as he slipped his hands into the pockets of his jeans and smiled at her.

"Riding? You mean actually riding on the racetrack?" Paige couldn't believe it. She had always wanted to do that. But the track and owners of horses worth thousands, and in some instances millions, of dollars didn't care to allow just anyone to ride the horses on the track.

"Will has a couple of horses he said we could ride. Jose has them all ready for us."

Paige squealed and leapt up into Cole's arms. This was so cool. When she was younger, she had wished she could be a jockey. However, her dreams were dashed when she reached five-feet-seven. But it never stopped her from dreaming of racing down the stretch toward the finish line.

They made their way past rows of white barns with green roofs until they reached the blue and white flag of Ashton Farm. As Cole had said, Will's barn manager was waiting for them. Two gorgeous chestnut horses were standing patiently while bits where being put into their mouths and blankets thrown over their backs. They were quickly saddled as Jose made introductions.

"Paige, you'll be riding Molly. And Cole, you'll be riding Polly. They're sisters and are getting ready to be bred next month. Will said you can run them today before they get transported back to the farm at the end of this week." Jose signaled the men holding the horses and waited for them to lead the horses one at a time to a hay bale.

Paige stepped onto the bale, lifted her left leg high in the air, and fit her foot into the stirrup. Molly stood still as Paige tightened her grip on her mane and swung her other foot over Molly's back. The freshly polished leather creaked as she settled into the saddle. She gently squeezed her thighs together and Molly instantly picked up on the cue and walked toward the track while Cole easily swung himself up on Polly.

A Keeneland security guard saw her coming and opened the gate onto the track. Paige glanced over her shoulder and found herself staring at the vision of Cole on top of a horse. He sat relaxed in the saddle as he confidently guided what looked to be a very happy Polly onto the racetrack.

Molly trotted out onto the track and Paige felt a sense of awe. Some of the best horses of all time had run on this track. Not only that, but it felt amazing. It may look like dirt, but the track was actually made of a synthetic blend called Polytrack. Molly's trot smoothed out as she hit the soft track and Paige clicked her tongue, urging Molly into a slow gallop.

"Let's take them around the track a couple of times at an easy gallop and then I challenge you to a race." Cole smirked as he pressed his heels into Polly's sides and guided her up into a gallop.

"You'll eat my dust, Parker!" Paige laughed as they set out around the iconic track.

"On your mark, get set, go!" Cole yelled. Paige squeezed her thighs and dug in with her heels. Molly shot from the line like the well-trained athlete that she was. Paige leaned over her neck, urging her to find her stride. She had slid into the rail as she watched Cole keeping pace with her on the outside.

"Come on, Molly!" she shouted. They rounded the half-mile marker and Paige gave Molly her head. Molly immediately sped up when Polly passed her on the outside. As they flew past the three-quarter-mile marker, Paige couldn't keep the smile from her face. This was the most fun she had had in years.

Cole was about a half-length in front of her as she squeezed Molly with her legs. Molly lunged forward and gained on Cole and Polly. Paige looked down the homestretch and took in the enormous empty grandstands and then turned her eye to the finish line. The power she felt in Molly as she thundered toward the finish line was indescribable.

Molly pushed harder and Paige could only hold on as Molly came neck and neck with Polly. In unison, they ate up the track trying to be the first across the finish line.

"Go, Molly!" Paige encouraged her as they made their final push across the finish line. The horses slowed, sweat turning their chestnut coats black.

"It was a dead heat. I would say we could do a half-mile sprint to determine a winner, but I am afraid I wouldn't win!" Cole laughed as he pulled Polly up next to her. "That, and we'd better get back to open the store." He leaned down and rubbed Polly's neck. "Did you have fun?"

"I had the best time. This was amazing! It was the most thoughtful thing anyone has done for me. I feel so alive! Thank you, Cole." Paige couldn't stop smiling as she dismounted from Molly. She would never forget how today felt.

★ ★ ★

Paige tried to focus on what she was doing, but her thoughts kept drifting to the man carrying in supplies from the storage room. Cole had talked to Salmond who recommended staying put, increasing gun presence inside the home, and placing undercover FBI outside the shop. Cole agreed and tried to make Paige feel more comfortable and safe with the added security. In the past week, Cole had taken her out on dates, made her dinner, and helped her in the store every day.

The store had been packed with people stopping by to get the latest on the shootings and the New York trial. Dani had been taken home under the cover of night and was doing well. Cole had even worked with Mo to set up a double date with them so Paige and Dani could see each other. Cole had also arranged for her to talk to Kenna who was safely ensconced at Cole's apartment.

All his actions showed someone who was caring and loving, not someone just pretending. They had a routine together, too. He'd walk Chuck while she showered. Then she'd make him breakfast and he'd make her lunch. He'd help her in the store and then he always thought of something for them to do together. Dinner in Lexington, renting a movie she'd wanted to see, or a visit to the comedy club. They were having so much fun she didn't want it to stop.

It had been quiet for a week. No faces in windows, no mysterious footsteps following them, and no shooting. She knew Cole had a real job to get back to. But she was so afraid that he wouldn't come back once he left. Paige was scared to death that this was only a fantasy and she wasn't ready to give it up yet. Especially since she knew she was in love with him.

They had fun days and amazing nights together, but Cole had never said this was anything but an assignment. They didn't talk about the future and never talked about their feelings. Unconsciously biting her lower lip, she knew it was up to her to make the first move. The fear of rejection hovered, though. She didn't know if she could take it if she was just part of his job. Was it better to put it all on the line and risk getting hurt? Or should she just keep it to herself and protect her heart?

"Heellooo?"

Paige jolted out of her thoughts and suppressed a groan when she raised her eyes and ran into two floatation devices stuffed into a children's tank top.

"Hi, Kandi. What can I do for you?"

"Aren't you going to say hi to Bill, too? I know you still pine for him and are sore about losing him, but you could at least be nice." Kandi rubbed her hand over Bill's chest but stopped short of rubbing his potbelly.

"Hi, Bill. I didn't see you behind Kandi's new coif. Now, what can I do for you, Kandi?"

"I am checking on all the businesses participating in the Summer Festival for the PTA. It looks like you have a lot of work to do. It doesn't look like you've done anything to prepare for it!" Kandi looked over her nose at the shop. Apparently she couldn't see over her nose or her giant beach balls to see the streamers, balloons, and beach gear put up around the shop.

"Oh. Didn't you see the decorations? Are your eyes okay? You may need to see someone about that. Cole helped me put them up. Didn't you, baby?" Paige mimicked Kandi and reached over to rub Cole's much broader muscled chest. She ran her fingers slowly over his defined abs and then smiled at Kandi.

"Hello, all! Oh, Paige, the place looks great!" Pam Gilford, in her pink polo shirt and knee-length khaki shorts, walked in with her clipboard. "I'll just check you off as ready to go for tomorrow."

"But," Kandi stammered, "there are hardly any decorations, and there are hardly any sale items. The display cases are empty!"

"Yes, and if you look right there, you can see that Cole just brought up four large boxes of what I am guessing are items for those display cases. Great job, you two."

"Pam, I am in charge of this Summer Festival and I will not tolerate mediocrity." Kandi stamped her heeled foot and glared at Pam.

"Yes, well, I am the president of the PTA and what I say goes." Pam paused and watched Chuck push open the partially open front door. "Well, look who is the mighty hunter!"

Chuck trotted in dragging a four-foot blacksnake, his tail happily wagging. Kandi's scream could have broken glass as she jumped behind Bill. The shriek was close enough to a dog whistle that Chuck thought Kandi was calling him. He wagged his big tail and headed straight for her. Kandi screamed again and jumped around Bill so Chuck couldn't get to her, which only started a game for him. Paige stood with a smile daring to break free as she watched Chuck and Kandi treat Bill like a merry-go-round.

"We should probably stop this," Cole said, but didn't move to stop Chuck.

"Yeah, probably." Paige watched as Bill went to grab Chuck who then thought it was a keep-away game, which caused his tail to wag even more. He was having a great time. Pam put her fingers in her mouth and let loose a shrill whistle. Everyone stopped where they were and stared at her.

"Chuck, come." She stood staring at Chuck with her hands on her knee-length khaki shorts. Chuck trotted over and sat down in front of her. She held out her hand. "Give." Chuck dropped the snake into her hand and thumped his tail on the ground. "Good boy."

"Eeew! That is a dead snake!" Kandi peeked out at the snake hanging from Pam's hand.

"Yup. Better than the two live ones my boys have. Anyway, place looks good. See you tomorrow!" Pam waved with the snake-less hand and headed out the door with the snake dangling from one hand and the clipboard in the other as the group stared open-mouthed at her.

★　　★　　★

Paige cleared the dishes from another of Cole's home-cooked dinners while he walked Chuck. They had talked at the table for hours and she felt more confused than ever. Yes, they had talked for hours but not about their relationship. They talked about growing up, their parents, high school, college, and her starting the shop. But not once did they talk about their future.

She placed the last dish in the dishwasher and closed the door. Cole came in through the back door with Chuck who immediately ran back to her bed to claim his spot. She turned off the lights after he locked the doors and checked the windows. She didn't know why, but the revelation of knowing she was in love with him had her feeling awkward whenever he became intimate with her. She was worried he'd get her so worked up, which he had a tendency to do. And in that moment of ecstasy, she'd scream out her love for him and that was not the way to tell someone how you truly felt.

They walked back to her bedroom and she couldn't help but fumble along. She needed to know what was going on between them before she got her heart broken. She stepped ahead of him and turned in the doorway.

"Well, um, thanks for dinner. It was great. Goodnight." She leaned forward and gave him a quick kiss on the lips and closed the door.

"Um, Paige?"

"Oh, of course!" She grabbed a pillow and opened the door. "Here you go. There are blankets on the couch. See you in the morning." She closed the door again and for good measure locked it.

Chapter Thirteen

The Summer Festival was in full swing. Paige smiled at the kids bounding around the street and into the stores lining Main Street. The sky was blue with puffy white clouds. A breeze helped to keep the humidity at tolerable levels. The balloons and laughter made it a perfect day. That morning she, Cole, and Betty Jo had moved tables out to the sidewalk. Paige chose the displays, Cole carried them to their destinations, and Betty Jo organized them.

Her summer hats were a big hit and she was selling enough to make room for the fall lineup she was working on. Paige scanned the crowd and stopped when a large red hat caught her attention. The crowd parted, either out of respect for the mistress of Wyatt Hall, or because Mrs. Wyatt smacked them with her cane.

"Mrs. Wyatt! It's so good to see you. Your hat matches your lipstick perfectly."

"Just like I wanted, thank you. This is my granddaughter, Katelyn Jacks." Paige looked up and up again. Katelyn was tall and gorgeous. She had to be just under six feet, with amazing, long blonde hair and cornflower-blue eyes. In the cute miniskirt she was wearing, Paige could see that her legs went on forever.

"It's so nice to meet you. You look like a model!"

"Thanks. I get that a lot." Katelyn held out her hand and shook Paige's.

"You get that a lot, dear, because you *are* a model." Mrs. Wyatt laughed.

"I *was* a model. I stopped modeling when I went to vet school."

Paige took another look at the long blonde hair, pulled back into a sleek ponytail, the sharp cheekbones, and startling blue eyes. "Well, if you ever miss it, I would love to have you model my hats for the magazines that keep calling. The *Town & Country* spread has really taken off and I had calls from tons of magazines. I have meetings with them next month to look over my fall line and pick out the hats they want to use in their spreads."

"Congratulations. What magazines have called you?"

"*Women's Wear Daily, Cosmo*, and *Glamour*," Paige said with pride.

"Wow! That is wonderful. I have shot for most of those before. I will probably know who you are working with. I would love to. I hated modeling, but it paid for college and grad school. But modeling for something like this would be great." Katelyn laughed and put an arm around her grandmother. "Actually, my favorite memory from growing up was playing in Grandma's hat room. The hats you have made for her these past four years are by far my favorites!"

"Thanks, Katelyn. I am so glad you have come to Keeneston. I know your grandparents love having you here and old Doc Truett is getting rather old. It will be good to have another vet here." Paige pointed out Chuck, who was trying to steal a cupcake off one of the tables. "That's my dog, Chuck. I will be sure to bring him by for his yearly when you get your practice up and running."

"Thanks. Jacks Animal Hospital should be up and running by next month." Katelyn smiled and Paige knew she had just made a new friend.

"Hey, Sis, where do you want me to put these pies Mom had me bring over for the contest?" Marshall strode up, balancing pies in his arms. "Mrs. Wyatt, looking good as always." He winked at her and gave her a quick kiss on the cheek.

"They go over there. But before you run off, let me introduce Katelyn Jacks. She's Mrs. Wyatt's granddaughter and a new Keeneston resident. She's also agreed to model my hats!"

"Jacks? As in the hotel heiress?"

"My father runs the hotels. I am not an heiress to anything."

Paige felt bad for Katelyn. It was obvious she was estranged from her very rich father and now her mother had run off with another husband. She'd worked hard to make something of herself and the first thing her idiot brother said was to identify her based on her father's accomplishments. He definitely deserved the icy stare she was giving him.

"So, you're a model. Figures. Welcome to Keeneston. See you later, Mrs. W." Marshall gave Mrs. Wyatt and wink and made his way to the pie table.

"I am sorry. My brothers don't have much tact. They're normally not assholes."

"I'm used to it. I just hope I can make my own name here."

Paige could kill her brother. The smile and relaxed attitude Katelyn had just a minute ago had been replaced by a self-conscious girl.

"I am sure you will be able to. We may know your family history back twelve generations, but we usually let people make their own names," Paige laughed.

"We'll let you get back to work. I am going to take Katelyn to meet Daisy, Violet, and Lily."

Paige gave Mrs. Wyatt a kiss and said her goodbyes to Katelyn before heading back into the shop.

"Hey, sweetheart. How are the sales going out here?" Cole came up behind her and wrapped his arms around her waist.

"Good. Just watched my brother make a jackass of himself in front of Mrs. Wyatt's granddaughter."

"What we men do for women," he chuckled. "I thought we could pack things up soon and then I would like to take you to the dance."

"Is it safe?"

"Yes. I just finished scoping it out. They are having it in a tent this year and it would be very hard to get a shot where they placed it."

"It sounds like fun. Just let me go change quickly." Cole turned her in his arms and gave her a quick kiss.

"I'll start moving things inside."

"Did I tell you how great you looked tonight?" Cole whispered into her ear as he led her into the dance. She had taken one of her own cowboy hats to wear tonight. Being inspired by Katelyn's miniskirt, Paige found a cute brown mini and matched it with an ivory, lace-trimmed tank top and cowboy boots.

"You have, but thank you."

Paige looked up at the top of the tent where the twinkle lights cast a romantic glow about the tent. Couples were already on the dance floor dancing to the music of the local bluegrass band that was currently playing "Blue Moon of Kentucky."

"Come on, let's go dance." Cole tugged her toward the dance floor.

"You know how to dance like this?"

"I wouldn't have asked you if I didn't know. Remember, I am a Southern boy. If my geography is right, Tennessee is farther south than Kentucky."

Paige let herself be pulled to the dance floor with a smile on her face. She loved to dance but rarely got to. The song ended as they reached the floor and a new song immediately started up. Cole grabbed her up and started dancing as the first twang of "I Am a Man of Constant Sorrow" started. He whirled her past other couples as if they had danced together their whole lives.

She felt her pulse beating to the banjo as he led her around the floor, holding her tight against his hard body. The tent was alive with laughter and music. There were frequent shouts and yee-haws as partners flew by one another. Paige tossed her head back and laughed as Cole twirled her around.

The lively song ended and Alison Krauss's "When You Say Nothing at All" slowed the crowd down. Couples stood and walked to the dance floor. Cole pulled her tighter and she laid her head against his shoulder. He took her hand and placed it over his heart as he rested his cheek against her head. Paige breathed him in and closed her eyes. The other couples disappeared and all she knew was how right they felt together. She lifted her head and looked up at him. His eyes were soft as he gazed down at her. She slid her arms around his neck as he leaned down and captured her lips with his. His tongue slowly slid into her mouth.

"May I cut in?" Paige's eyes snapped open. Cole didn't loosen his hold on her, only looked for confirmation from Paige.

"Sure." Cole let go of her then and gave Miles a slight nod of acknowledgment. "I'll go get us some drinks." Paige watched as Cole walked off the dance floor and then turned to her big brother.

"Do you all have to butt in constantly? Look. I love you all, but I am getting to a point where we're going to have major issues if you don't quit interfering in my personal life."

Her brother infuriated her by only shrugging. "You look nice tonight, Sis." Paige's anger fell away as Miles danced the rest of the song with her. "Mom and Dad are here tonight, too, and just saw your make-out session on the dance floor. Dad was going to come, but Mom sent me. I am to invite the two of you to a family dinner tomorrow night."

"Uh-oh."

"Yup. He's being called in for the formal interview."

"But we're not even a couple. I mean, our relationship is fake."

"It looked pretty real to me. See you tomorrow, Sis." Miles kissed her on the forehead and headed to report back to their parents.

"Everything okay?" Cole asked as he brought her some lemonade.

"Yeah. We've been invited to dinner tomorrow night at my parents."

"Great. Come on, this is one of my favorite songs."

"The Devil Went Down to Georgia?"

"Sure is. I bet you'll be having the time of your life dancing to this song!"

Boots stamped, hands clapped, and Paige did have the time of her life.

★　　★　　★

Cole pulled up to her parents' farmhouse and turned off the engine. Alerted by the sound of the car door closing, her family came out to the wraparound porch to meet them. Everyone but Cy made it to family dinner, especially when summoned by Mom. The last man she had brought out for family dinner was Bill and it had been a disaster.

Bill had been shocked by her tomboy ways, insulted at the informal, loud, boisterous dinner, and not amused by her brothers' continuous questions. He had said a quick goodbye and headed home as soon as dessert was over. One week later he was boinking Kandi.

Cole waved to her family and came around the car to open her door. He had dressed in khaki pants and a French-blue dress shirt that made his silver eyes look ice-blue. She smiled as he helped her out of the truck and wondered why it was her hands that were sweaty and not Cole's.

"Thanks for inviting me to dinner, Mrs. Davies." Paige watched her mother fluster as Cole gave her his full smile before turning to her father. "Mr. Davies." He shook her father's hand.

"Nice grip, son. Not one of those pansy handshakes. Come on and take a seat. We were just about to have a beer. Would you like one?" Her father gestured to the long row of rocking chairs on the front porch.

"Sounds good." Cole turned and gave her a quick look to make sure he didn't need to stay with her. When she gave a slight nod, he took the offered beer and had a seat among her father and brothers.

"Come help me get dinner on the table, dear." Her mother gently ushered her into the house. "I have a feeling he'll be just fine."

"Right. Dad and the boys have a history of being nice to my dates."

"Date? I thought he was just your security."

Damn. Her mom saw way too much. "Um, right." Smooth, Paige, real smooth.

"Here, put these plates on the table and then call the boys in for dinner."

Paige set the table and called the men in to dinner. Her mother had made fried chicken and sweet potato casserole for dinner along with bread and a salad. Everyone hurried in and took their customary seats. Her mother had set an extra place next to Paige and she watched as he moved comfortably around her family to take his seat.

Her mother led grace, and Paige threw in an extra prayer for good luck. As soon as the amens were said, the moment Paige had been dreading happened. Her father set his fork down on his plate and laced his fingers together. He stared right at Cole who was innocently taking a bite of his chicken.

"So tell me, Cole, what are your intentions with our Paige?" Paige groaned and sat back in her chair. It was no use trying to fight it. She was just going to watch the evening go down in flames and prepare herself for the inevitable "It's been great, but" speech from Cole tomorrow.

"Well, I intend to keep her safe until this man is caught."

"It seems that your job may be at an end, Cole. With the indictment, it's been quiet for over a week. I bet you're itching to get back to your life now — and your own apartment." Miles took another bite of dinner, never taking his eyes off Cole.

"You all should know better than that. It's the quiet times I worry about the most." Cole looked at her mother and smiled. "These potatoes are really great, Mrs. Davies."

"Thank you, Cole. You can call me Marcy." Well, at least he had gotten her mother's approval. That was more than Bill had gotten.

"I have an idea. Did you know my big sis is a great shot? Why don't we have a tournament after dinner, just like we used to?" Pierce smiled at her so sweetly that she narrowed her eyes. What was he up to? She was an excellent shot and very competitive. She would excel at this, so what was his point?

"So, Cole, you ever play any sports?" Cade asked.

"Yes. I played football in high school and college."

"What position?"

"Mostly receiver. How do you enjoy coaching?"

"I like it a lot. We're pretty inexperienced this season, but with Will coaching, I think we'll do pretty well. Have a couple of seniors that are getting a lot of looks from colleges. Paige here is one of our biggest fans. She doesn't miss a game. She's kinda competitive. If I were less of a man, I might be embarrassed." Cade winked at her.

Yea! Cade approved. She blushed at his teasing, though. Okay, so she really got into the game, but that didn't mean all her brothers had to laugh at her like they were doing now. Snickering behind their napkins. Oh, she'd show them after dinner.

"Come on, Pierce, let's go get the targets set up." Her father placed his napkin on the table and headed out to the back yard.

"Marshall, get a rifle for Cole. I am going to get one of my extras from my room." Paige stood up from the table and put down her napkin.

"Extras? Where's your primary one?" Cole asked.

"In my truck. Where else?" She turned on her heel and headed up to her room.

"Sorry, little bro. Maybe you'll beat me when I am old and my eyesight is gone." Miles patted Pierce's head and laughed.

"Too bad the military didn't teach you how to shoot." Paige crowed to Marshall. The first round was five shots at one hundred yards with no scopes. All five of her rounds were bull's-eyes.

"Sorry, Mr. Davies, but a tournament's a tournament." Cole smiled and shook her father's hand.

"You can call me Jake. Good luck, you'll need it." Paige smiled. Now if only her brothers could get on board.

"Cade, you take Paige. Miles, you and Cole go together." Her father moved the targets back fifty yards and moved far off to the side. At his signal Miles shot, then Cade. Her father collected the targets and put new ones up. Paige shot and then Cole.

"Sweet pea versus hot-shot FBI agent," her father shouted as he moved the targets back another fifty yards.

"Good shooting, Parker. You're the first one to knock Miles out besides Paige. Where'd you learn to shoot like that?" Paige smiled; Marshall was on board now.

"Oh, didn't I mention I started off as a sniper for the FBI?"

"Oh, you got us!" Pierce laughed and slapped him on the back. Miles was the last holdout.

"Ladies first." Cole swept his arm to the line.

Paige took her aim and gently squeezed the trigger. She made a minor adjustment and gently squeezed off four more shots. Cole stepped up to the line and waited for her father to wave the "all clear." He aimed and squeezed off his five shots.

They watched as her father took down his target and compared the two as he walked back to the group.

"Sorry, gentlemen, lady's the winner — again." Her father shook his head as he held up the two targets.

"Wow. It was close. Great job, sweetheart." Cole pulled her near and gave her a kiss on her head in front of her whole family.

"Come have a beer with us, Cole." Miles thumped him on the back. He'd passed all the tests.

"I would love to, but I really need to run to my apartment and get some things. Can you all watch Paige and I will be back in an hour to take her home? I figured that would give her enough time to rub it in that she beat us all."

Chapter Fourteen

Paige hugged her parents and waved goodbye to her brothers as she got into Cole's Explorer. She watched as Cole shook her father and brothers' hands, and then gave her mother a hug before walking around to his side of the car. If only she knew that tonight had a future, she'd be the happiest person alive.

"Your family is great."

"Even during the interrogation?"

"Yes, even during the interrogation. It just shows how much they love you and that's really special."

"You don't mind the competitiveness?"

"No. I loved it. You're a great shot by the way. How did you become so good? I was at the top of my class at the Academy and you beat me." Paige was slightly embarrassed by the praise but was really proud. She had worked hard and her brothers had supported her all the way. But most men were intimidated and didn't like being beaten by a girl.

"It didn't bother you that I beat you?"

"No. Why would it?"

"Because I am a girl."

"Again, why would that bother me? I know lots of girls who are better than I'm at certain things."

"Just in the past, guys I dated were bothered when I beat them at sports."

"Then they were just insecure and jealous that you were better than they were. You didn't answer my question. How did you get so good?"

"I followed my big brothers around everywhere. I wanted to be just like them. I started shooting as soon as I was big enough to hold a rifle. My father started taking me to target practice with them when I got big enough. My brothers were nice enough to let me tag along. They encouraged me and taught me how to read the wind and the physics of shooting.

"They also got a kick out of challenging their friends and watching me beat them. They didn't take it as well as you did, especially when they were between fifteen and seventeen years old and I was just ten. They told me to play my own game and take my own shot. It never bothered me until I was older and wanted to date guys. They were intimidated by my being better at shooting, football, and basketball. You add very overprotective brothers into the mix and you get a very boring social life."

Cole pulled into the back of her shop and opened her door. He held out his hand and she slipped hers into his. His thumb traced small circles over her pulse point on her wrist as he led her up the stairs.

"You know, I think it's pretty hot that you're good at all those things." Cole unlocked the door and turned off the new alarm.

"You do?"

"Yeah." Cole pulled her against him and brushed her hair away from her face. "Let me show you just how hot I find you."

Oh boy.

Paige awoke to the banging of pots in the kitchen. She reached over looking for Cole, but only encountered a furry, snoring Chuck. What had she done? She'd had amazing sex, duh. But, no! She had made a deal with herself not to do that anymore. It would only make it harder when he left. She was already in over her head with her feelings. She didn't need fabulous sex to cloud her judgment.

"Okay. No more sex. No more kissing. No more really, really, really great sex," she told Chuck who just thumped his tree trunk of a tail.

She tugged on a pair of olive shorts and pulled out a white ribbed shirt from her drawers. She pulled open her door and headed down the hall for the kitchen. When she walked through the living room, she spotted boxes piled up and the kitchen door open.

"What's going on?" she asked Cole as he carried another box in from his car.

"Morning, sweetheart! I brought some things from my house."

"But those are pots and pans. And that box is labeled linens. I have all those things. I don't understand." Paige looked at the box marked "kitchen" and found a blender and some Tupperware.

"Well, I didn't know how long I would be here for this case, so I decided to bring some of my favorite things from home to use. And, guess what? I got you something!" Cole reached behind the island and pulled out a red vacuum cleaner. "Isn't it great? It even picks up dog hair."

Paige stared at the red vacuum, speechless. Lingerie, flowers, chocolates, a picture frame. Those would be acceptable gifts. But, a vacuum? For as long as the case goes on? Oh. No. He. Didn't.

"What do you think?" Cole asked. She looked away from the vacuum and saw him move over her toaster and plug in his blender. Her pots were being stacked up to make room for a skillet and a George Foreman grill. "Well?"

"You got me a vacuum? What was wrong with the vacuum I had?"

"Well, this one picks up dog hair. I thought you could use it on the couch and then we wouldn't have Chuck hair all over our clothes." He smiled as if he had just given her a diamond ring.

"Are you an idiot?" Paige put her hands on her hips and stared at Cole as he unpacked a quesadilla maker.

"Huh?" She watched as his eyebrows came together in confusion.

"What are you doing? Why are you unpacking all this… this stuff? Because it looks like you're moving in."

"Well, I am."

"You are? I don't remember having this discussion. I don't recall you asking me if this is what I wanted. Actually, come to think of it I don't recall us even having a real relationship."

"Of course we have a relationship. What do you think we've been doing for the past month?"

"Well, as far as we have talked about, you've been protecting me and acting in a fake relationship." She felt her face flush in anger over his presumptions.

"But we're sleeping together," Cole said as if that explained the whole situation.

"Oh, I know we're sleeping together. Having sex doesn't mean we have a relationship and that you can just move all your stuff in without talking to me about it!" Paige threw her hands up in the air. "And then you get me a vacuum. A vacuum!"

"What's wrong with the vacuum? It picks up pet hair," Cole bit out.

"Arg!" Unbelievable! He just didn't get it. You can't go from never talking about a relationship, to moving in without asking, and then to bringing a vacuum as a gift.

She was speechless. But the words working their way out of her mouth were lost. She grabbed the keys to her truck and with a glare, ran past Cole down the backstairs to her truck. She needed to get away. She needed a moment of quiet to think this over and to scream at the top of her lungs. She ignored Cole as he yelled at her to stop from the top of the stairs. Paige unlocked her truck and shoved the key in the ignition.

"Paige! Stop! Don't you dare leave here. Get back here this instant!" Cole yelled as he raced down the stairs.

"Oh, I double-dog dare you… you vacuum gifter!" She cranked over the key and slammed the truck into reverse and laid rubber.

Angry tears streamed down her face as she drove toward her parents' house. A vacuum! As if she was the happy little woman of the house cleaning up the dog hair so it wouldn't get on his shirt. Nooo, that would imply they had a talk to determine she was the woman of the house.

Maybe Miss Lily had been right all these years. Why buy the cow when you can get the milk for free. They have some great, really great sex and he thought she was a vacuum type girl. No words of love, no relationship determination, just a vacuum. Well, he could just take that vacuum and shove it up his…

"Crap." Paige slammed on the brakes and did a controlled slide onto the dirt road. She pressed the gas pedal down as she bounced down the road toward her sanctuary.

Paige drove past the cornfields and her brothers' cows that used some of her parents' empty fields. She looked in her rearview mirror and saw nothing but a cloud of dust as she made her way to the field connected to the woods. Passing the last row of corn, she slammed on the brakes and slid to a stop.

A vacuum! A freaking vacuum! She threw the gearshift into Park and hopped out, leaving the keys dangling in the ignition. She slammed the door and stalked her way across the field on the path to the rocks. She didn't notice the hot, humid air or the noise from the cicadas. Nope, all she could think about was that red vacuum cleaner.

"But it picks up dog hair." Ah! And he had a whole box of bed linens. Like he was ever going to get back into her bed. Nope. Those linens would look great on the couch. He could stay there for the rest of his life for all she cared. Wait. Whole life? No sir, they hadn't talked about "whole life". He had only talked about the duration of the case.

Paige made it to the woods and stopped. She looked around the peaceful, wooded path and turned to look out across the field and screamed, "Freakin' vacuum cleaner! He got me a freakin' vacuum cleaner!" She turned back down the path and started a quick walk down the half-mile trail.

Paige jumped from the downed tree onto the rocks. She dropped to her knees and cried for all she was worth. She didn't want to be the vacuum cleaner type. She wanted to be the sexy lingerie type. She'd even settle for a cute little pistol. They could be sexy if he got the right one. But you couldn't make a vacuum sexy. So she cried. The man she loved found her as sexy as a vacuum that picked up dog hair.

Eventually she got tired of crying and sat up. She was covered in tears, sweaty from stomping down the path, and just plain worn out from crying. She kicked off her shoes and dangled her bare feet over the rock and into the creek. Oh, the cool water felt so good. With a sigh, she stood up and started to walk around in the creek. Her feet sunk slightly into the soft bottom. The babbling of the water soothed her as she breathed in the fresh air, listened to the birds chirping, and heard the gentle breeze playing music with the leaves.

Why did she have to love him so much? Why did he have to be so happy when he showed her all his stuff? And why did he have to look so confused when she got upset? He was so happy when he showed her the vacuum as if he put a lot of thought into it. As if he thought the gift was something she'd really love. He looked so expectant.

Oh no. Did she overreact? Was the vacuum and moving in his way of telling her he loved her and wanted a relationship? Why do that when he could have just told her? Maybe he didn't know how or maybe he was too scared to say those three words. After all, she had been too scared to say those three words. If he was too scared, she wasn't. Not anymore. She had to tell him what she felt.

She took another deep breath and knew this is what she needed to do. She skimmed her fingers along the top of the flowing water and made up her mind to get out of the creek, walk to the truck, and drive back home to tell Cole she loved him and wanted him to move in with her. After all, how many guys could win the support of her whole family? Paige smiled with determination. She turned and started walking back to the rocks through the knee-high water.

She had almost reached the rocks when she heard a twig snap in the woods. She turned her head in the direction of noise. It had come from the path. Cole had come after her! She could tell him how much she loved him now.

"Cole! Oh, I am so glad you're here. Look, I am so sorry for our fight this afternoon. I shouldn't have reacted like that when I found out you got me a vacuum. I am sure it's a lovely vacuum, but it's just that I have something to tell you. I love you. I love you with all my heart and all my soul. I want you to stay with me, vacuum and all. Please tell me you will. Please tell me you will stay with me and try to love me as much as I love you." She had reached the rocks and was about to pull herself up when a face came into view, a face that had been haunting her dreams.

"He got you a vacuum? What an idiot." The assassin raised his rifle and aimed it right at her head.

Paige didn't have time to scream. Her heart lodged in her throat preventing any noise from coming out. She dove downstream as the bullet whizzed by her head and lodged in the tree behind her. The cold water washed over her head as her body slammed into the soft creek bottom. As she pushed up, her hands sunk into the silt and she gasped for air. She heard him fighting the brush surrounding the creek and got to her knees. She crawled to the side of the creek where the bottom was harder, then got to her feet.

Her breaths came in short gasps as she looked back and saw him hacking his way through the vegetation to get a clear shot. Not thinking twice, she took off running down the creek. Her legs ached as they pushed against the water and against the creek bed that was trying to swallow her feet. She couldn't hear anything except the water being splashed around by her legs.

She hadn't made it ten yards when she heard him break through the brush and jump into the creek after her. She turned back and saw him desperately pulling at his legs to get them out of the silt. He was stuck in the creek bed! He raised his rifle again and took aim. Paige darted to her right as the shot went wide. She just had to make it five more feet to the bend in the creek. She pushed herself as she zigzagged to safety. She took one last look back as she saw him pull one of his legs free.

She rounded the bend and made her way to the left side of the creek. There was a deer trail a couple of feet away. She could follow that to the main path and then to her truck. She looked up at the opening in the briars and hoped like hell she could make it up the bank to the deer trail. She fell against the muddy bank and tried to get traction as she looked at the lip about four feet over her head. Her bare feet slipped on the mud as she tried to climb up. Her nails clawed frantically at the mud trying to find a hold. She looked around and saw that a briar bush hung down along the bank next to her. Not letting herself think, she grabbed as high as she could as the sharp thorns sank into her palms.

The thorns ripped skin as she pulled her hand from the bush. She grabbed the grass, causing briars left in her palm to dig in deeper. She grimaced and clawed along the grass until she was able to pull herself all the way up.

She didn't allow herself any time to think. She pushed herself to her feet and took off at a dead run toward her truck. Her bare feet hit the ground hard as she ran. Twigs broke under her feet and splinters, thorns, and mud stuck to her as she pushed herself along the tiny trail.

Paige leapt over a downed tree and fell onto the main path. Her bare feet momentarily slipped on the dry dirt. She caught herself and cried out as her hand slammed against a tree. She righted herself and started jogging down the lane.

"Didn't anybody teach you to never leave your keys in the car?" She looked back in time to see him round the corner about sixty yards behind her. He took a couple wild shots and she pushed herself to sprint the remaining quarter-mile.

If she could only make it to her truck. He might have the keys, but he probably didn't have the rifle hidden in the back seat. The trouble was making it all the way across the field. He was gaining on her and she didn't know if she could make it to her truck.

Paige saw the sunlight in the field ahead of her. The trees thinned as she broke out of the woods. Her lungs burned and her feet were numb. She kept her eyes locked on the truck as she noticed the dirt in the air behind it. She was only halfway there when she saw Cole's Explorer pulling into the field. She frantically looked behind her in time to see him drop to a knee and take aim.

The shot reverberated on the trees and floated through the field. Cole's windshield cracked as the bullet pierced the glass. Paige didn't stop running as Cole slammed on the brakes and pulled his car sideways, the passenger seat door closest to her. She heard more gunfire and glass shattering as Cole wrenched open the driver's door and rolled out of the car.

She was only fifteen yards from her truck now. Cole returned fire, pinning the assassin to the tree line one hundred fifty yards away. Paige pushed herself harder as she skidded over the hood and landed hard on the ground. Shots ricocheted off her truck as she reached for the door. Crouching, she opened the driver's door and pushed the seat forward. Glass rained down on her as bullets shattered the windshield. She threw her arms over her head as tiny fragments of glass bit into her exposed arms.

Cole returned fire and she lunged for the black rifle bag on the floor in the backseat. She unzipped the bag and pulled out her Browning BAR Mark II rifle. She loaded it as volleys of gunfire surrounded her. She took a deep breath and slowly let it out to steady herself. She stood and placed the rifle barrel on the dashboard where her windshield used to be.

Lowering her head to the sight, she narrowed the world to a tiny circle on his chest. She quickly adjusted for the wind and distance before taking in a deep breath and letting it out slowly. The trigger lay gently against the pad of her finger as she applied just enough pressure to fire. Never taking her eye off the target, she watched as her bullet hit the target at the same time Cole fired. The rifle dropped from the assassin's hand as he fell to the ground.

Chapter Fifteen

Paige decided she had seen too many horror movies in her life. All she could think about was the bimbo who shot the bad guy, then dropped her weapon as she went to see if he was still alive. The bimbo would be hysterical and not notice the villain's finger twitch. Then the bimbo would need to get real close to see if the villain was breathing. She put her face inches from the villain's and then was surprised when his eyes popped open and he grabbed her. She refused to be that bimbo.

She held on to her weapon, letting Cole check to see if he was breathing. Paige glanced quickly to her right to see that Cole was calling in the situation. She kept her gun leveled on the assassin as she stepped around the truck.

"Stay there, Paige!" Cole yelled as he hung up the phone and shoved it in the back pocket of his jeans.

"Like hell! But I will let you go first!" Paige screamed across the field as she slowly walked toward the man.

She watched Cole take the lead with his pistol drawn and aimed at the man on the ground. He stopped about five feet away and looked down at him. She kept her rifle raised and took position slightly behind Cole and to his left. Cole nodded his head toward the gun and she picked up on the signal. She slid over and kicked the gun out of the reach of the man.

"He's been hit twice," Cole told her.

"I got him in his right shoulder," Paige informed him.

"And I got him in his left." Cole smiled and gave her a wink, but she was too focused on the man's fingers. Did they just move? She would swear they moved.

"Cole, be careful. I would have sworn his fingers just moved." Paige kept her eyes on the man's hand as Cole got closer to him.

"So?"

"I don't want you to be the bimbo."

Cole lowered his gun and stared at her. "What in the hell does that mean? Why would I be a bimbo?"

"Well, everyone knows that in the movies the bimbo drops her guard when she assumes the villain is dead and that's when he attacks. Duh." Paige rolled her eyes. Bless his heart, shouldn't he know that as an FBI agent?

"Honey, don't you have enough faith in my abilities to beat a man with two gunshot wounds if he attacks me now?" Cole's eyebrows rose cockily as he stared her down.

"That was before you bought me a vacuum. Just be careful."

Cole edged forward with his gun raised. He stopped when he stood over the man and looked down on him. Paige watched as he nudged his hand with the toe of his brown work boot.

"Looks like he's unconscious. You got a clean shot to the shoulder. That was a nice shot, sweetheart. Just don't ever do it again. Do you know what it does to a man to see the woman he loves running from an assassin who is shooting at her? It took ten years off my life."

"What it does to you?" Paige forgot about the bimbo in the movies and lowered her gun as her hands went to her hips. She stared him down with a shocked expression as she tried to figure out if he really was lecturing her. Yes, she decided, he was. "Did you think about what it does to me? It's not like I do this for a living. But, that's beside the point. I did do it and I did it well. I can take care of myself, thank you very much."

Cole opened his mouth, but nothing came out. Paige looked up into the sky and thought about what he had said to her. She felt as if she missed something. Clean shot to shoulder. Good shot. Don't do it again. Ten years. Love you. Love you! Wait, what?

"Did you say you love me?" Paige couldn't decide if she was embarrassed for asking or just nervous for his answer. Either way, she felt her face flush and her heart beat rapidly against her chest. She was afraid to blink because she might miss his answer.

"Yeah, I said 'I love you.' I have loved you for months. I was just too stubborn to admit to myself that I needed you." Paige felt tears well up in her eyes and took a step toward Cole.

"Shit!" she screamed.

"Um, okay. That was not the response I was expecting." Cole's smile faded and he took a sudden interest in the unconscious man at his feet.

"No. Not you. Sorry, wait!" Paige screamed as he started to turn away and walk back to the truck. "That didn't sound right. I stepped on another thistle and it really hurt. I was going to come to you, but you may just have to come to me." Paige looked down at her bloodied feet and wiggled her toes. Ewww, a couple of her toenails were gone.

Cole turned and saw her wiggling her bloodied toes. Paige saw the second he comprehended that she was injured. His face went from red to white as he ran over to her.

"What in the hell is this?"

"Um, feet?"

"You didn't have shoes? This whole time you were injured and you didn't tell me? Dammit, Paige, I told you to wait at the truck, but did you listen? Oh no, Paige Davies could never listen to anyone!"

"Cole."

"What!"

"Shut up and tell me you love me."

Cole raised his eyes from her damaged feet and holstered his gun. "I love you more than anything else in this world… your stupidity and all." He gave her a wink and she let out a squeak as he scooped her up in his arms.

"Ooh, that feels so much better. But I refuse to be the bimbo." Paige rested the gun on Cole's shoulder and kept it aimed at the man.

"Fine. Refuse to be the bimbo all the way until I take you to the hospital. But then you kind of have to put away the gun." Cole kissed her wrinkled brow.

"Hospital! I don't need a hospital. Just some tweezers and peroxide." Cole raised one eyebrow at her and glanced down at her feet. Paige wanted to stick out her tongue. But she looked down at her feet and the blood slowly dripping to the ground. Thorns stuck out everywhere and deep cuts ran along the tops and bottoms of her heel. Toenails were ripped off and bleeding. Well, maybe she might need to go to the hospital, but she'd be damned if she'd admit it!

"You just realized you need to go to the hospital, didn't you?" Cole smirked.

Paige responded by sticking out her tongue.

"You're so cute when you do that." Cole leaned forward and kissed her with all his worry, anxiety, and love put into the one kiss.

"Jesus, Parker. Put my sister down. This is not the time to be making out with her. There is a bleeding, unconscious man on the ground and she's holding a gun." Pierce stood next to his father, both holding their hunting rifles and staring at them with cold, hard looks.

From where they stood, they could only see her back and her feet were out of view. As if thinking the same thing, Cole turned so they could see.

"I am sure you can appreciate why I am holding your sister and why I refuse to put her down." Cole looked down at her feet and Paige watched as the other two men fixed their gaze on her mangled feet.

"Oh, sweet pea, what happened?" Her father asked as he rushed over to her.

"I was down at the rocks when I heard someone coming. I thought it was Cole, so I didn't bother to hide. But, it was him," she gestured to the man still unconscious on the ground. "Then he fired at me and I dove into the water and ran downstream until I was able to claw my way out and up to a deer trail. I ran barefoot down the deer path to the main trail and then across the field to my truck while the man fired on Cole. I made it to my truck and got Sally out. I got a shot in his right shoulder while Cole shot him in the left."

"And where were you while she was by herself at the creek? I thought the whole purpose of you staying with Paige at the shop and her apartment was to guard her. Now, the one time she needs you, you aren't here until it was almost too late!" Pierce's face was starting to get red and it was easy to forget he was only twenty-two-years old.

"Pierce, it was my fault. I got upset about something and stormed out before he could stop me. Cole raced after me and tried to stop me, but I didn't listen. I am just glad he knew where to find me."

"What did you do, son?" her father asked Cole.

"How did you know it was me?"

"It's always you. Haven't you learned that yet?"

Paige tried not to snicker at Cole's face. His lips formed a tight line and he looked like he was trying to figure out how and when something went wrong. Poor guy, it would always be his fault.

"He got me a gift." Paige handed off her gun to her brother and crossed her arms over her chest as she stared Cole down.

"I don't get it, sir. I got her a gift and she got madder than a hornet's nest at me." Cole pleaded his case to her father. "It is a top-of-the-line vacuum cleaner that is specially made to pick up dog hair. It even comes with a five-year warranty." Cole's plea got cut off by her father's bark of laughter.

"Oh boy, you were fixin' to get into it, weren't you? You never buy a woman an appliance or anything to use for keeping house. I reckon you won't be doing that again, now will you?"

"It would have been helpful to know that before I gave her the vacuum," Cole mumbled.

"Don't feel bad, son. I gave Marcy a new iron for Christmas when we were first married. My head still aches when rain is comin' on."

"Daddy! Mom would never hit you with an iron!" Paige laughed and temporarily forgot about the pain in her feet.

"If you could have easily picked up the vacuum and swung it at Cole's head, you would have." Her father paused to let her think for a second. When she tried to fight the smile tugging on her mouth, he just nodded his head. "Your mother has quite the arm."

Paige wondered how Cole could hold her for so long. Police, EMTs, and Ahmed swarmed the field. The abrasive noise, lights, and fumes transformed the quiet field into a nightmare. All she wanted was quiet. She wanted to take a deep breath and let the country air heal her. Cole kept her wrapped up in his arms as he talked to everyone who responded, issuing orders on how he wanted the situation handled.

"Ahmed!" Cole yelled when he saw Ahmed close his phone.

"How are you, Paige?" Ahmed asked, his cold mask always intact.

"I'll live, but I don't think I will be wearing my heels anytime soon."

With something that might have been a twitch to his lip, Ahmed looked at Cole.

"I need a favor," Cole said. "Well, two actually."

Ahmed didn't bother answering. He gave a barely perceivable nod of acknowledgment. "I want you to watch over him. When he wakes up, scare the crap out of him. Hopefully, that will get him to talk to me."

"I can handle that. I'll ride over in the ambulance with him and get to him as soon as he wakes up. However, we'll want our own words with him. What's the second favor?"

"Both our cars are shot up and I need to get Paige to the hospital to have her feet cleaned up. Can I use your car?" Ahmed reached into his pocket, pulled out his keys, and tossed them to Cole.

"Which car is yours?" Paige sarcastically asked as she glanced around the field. The shiny black Mercedes looked alien sitting in the middle of the field, surrounded by mud-splattered SUVs and pickup trucks.

"Jake, Pierce, I am going to take her to the hospital to get cleaned up. Can you look in our cars and get whatever we might need out of them before they get towed into evidence?"

"Sure." Her father gave her a kiss on the cheek and smiled down at her. "Take care of yourself. We'll be over tomorrow to check on you. You know your mother, she'll be baking for the rest of the night when I tell her what happened. Get some rest. She'll be a force to reckon with tomorrow."

"Thanks, Daddy. I love you."

"Love you too, sweet pea." Paige started to tear up as she watched her father and brother retrieve her purse from her car. Her gun had already been turned over to the police as evidence.

"It's okay, sweetheart. Everything is okay now." Cole placed a lingering kiss on her forehead and walked to Ahmed's car.

Paige watched the University of Kentucky's campus come into view as they drove up South Limestone. Her head rested against the soft leather as she watched an empty Commonwealth Stadium fly by. In just a couple of weeks, the stadium would be packed for the first football game of the season, but now it sat patiently waiting for game day.

She knew how it felt. Cole was right; everything was okay now. There was no one trying to kill her, which meant no reason for Cole to stick around. What was going to happen now that they would be forced into the real world? A world with Cole living in Lexington and her in Keeneston. A world where Cole placed himself in danger every day. How would it all work?

The large hospital complex drew closer as Cole turned into the emergency entrance. "Stay here. I'll get a wheelchair for you."

"I can't really run off now, can I?"

"I don't know. You might be stubborn enough to try."

As Paige watched him stride into the hospital, she knew they weren't just talking about her feet.

Chapter Sixteen

Paige felt her temper start to rise. She was independent and hated to be treated like she was a child. She was behind the curtain in one of the emergency bays. The nurse had handed her a set of scrubs to change into. Her wet clothes were turning cold in the air conditioning and she was freezing, not counting filthy. The nurse had taken a pair of scissors to the bottoms of the scrubs to turn them into shorts so they could get to all the cuts and scrapes on her legs to clean and stitch them.

The problem was the mother hen in the room with her. He was smothering her. She went to peel off her wet t-shirt and he jumped up and tried to help her. In actuality, the only thing he did was get in her way.

She stopped herself from snapping at him because she knew he was so concerned for her. But she secretly hoped the nurse would kick him out when she got back.

"Cole, just let me do this," she begged.

"No, you're hurt." It appeared Cole was determined.

Paige rolled her eyes as her arms were raised and Cole had the t-shirt pulled over her head so she couldn't see anything. She almost cheered when she heard his cell phone ring. He cursed, as he clearly couldn't answer it while trying to take off her shirt.

"I've got this. Just answer your phone. It could be important." Paige yanked her arms away from Cole and peeled off her wet shirt in one yank. Before Cole could get off the phone, she stripped off her shorts and slipped on the dry scrubs.

"That was Mo. He's upstairs in the physical therapy room with Dani and a lot of guards. After you get your feet fixed up, I will take you up there and leave you with Dani. Mo wanted to talk to me about the assassin. I will go check on him while you and Dani have a chance to see each other."

Paige gritted her teeth and tried not show how pissed off she really was, but it was hard. She hated being pushed around in one of those God-awful blue plastic wheelchairs by someone who was treating Paige like a two-year-old. Wasn't it she who evaded and then shot the assassin?

Now Cole was treating her as if she couldn't sit at the big boys' table. Paige had asked if she could be included in his talks with Mo, but he said no with this little smile on his face that she wished she could wipe off. Cole had told her that Mo didn't want to worry Dani. These boys were clueless. She stopped grinding her teeth and knew she just needed to bide her time. She and Dani would find out what was going on even if the boys thought they didn't need to know.

Cole turned down a hall and walked right into a wall of bodyguards. Paige looked up and smiled as Cole told them who they were. One no-neck man knocked on a door. When it opened, he whispered something to the occupant. The door closed for a second and then reopened as Mo appeared.

"Paige, I am so glad you are okay. Please let me know if you need anything. Dani is excited she's getting to see you." With a nod of his head, Cole pushed her to the door and let a guard open it.

"Don't worry, I can wheel myself in. Where are you boys going to be?" Paige tried for casual and hoped they didn't catch on to her snooping.

"We'll be right out here for the next couple of minutes. Then we're heading down to the ICU. If you need us, just let one of the guards know and they'll come get us," Cole told her as he let go of her wheelchair.

She looked back and saw both of them standing right behind her watching as she made her way into the room. She moved slowly and hoped they really were so impatient to talk to each other they wouldn't see what she was doing, or what she wasn't going to do. She smiled at them and slowly moved through the door.

"I got it from here, thank you," she told Mr. No-Neck. He stepped out of her way and she put a hand on the door as she wheeled through.

"Paige!" Dani jumped up from a mat on the floor and rushed over. "I was wondering who was coming in the door! I told Mo I had to see you before I believed you were okay."

Perfect. Dani was talking loud enough for everyone in the hall to hear.

"You're looking good, Dani. Can you a help a girl out with the door?" She gave her a wink and a smile. Dani's smile grew as she picked up on the plan instantly. Dani held open the door and gave the men in the hall a quick wave. Paige rolled through the door and Dani closed the door so the latch rested against the frame. The result was a small crack that made it easy to eavesdrop. With a grin to each other, Dani helped Paige out of her wheelchair and up to the crack in the door.

"Do we know who this man is yet?" Mo asked Cole.

"Not yet. The prints we ran came back with several identities, just like the description. Apparently our man covers his tracks well and has multiple identities good enough to fool authorities." She heard Cole sigh and knew that he was running his hand through his hair like he always did when he was frustrated.

"Why was he in the system?"

"It was all traffic. Nothing more than speeding tickets and a couple parking tickets."

"What are your plans? You had asked for Ahmed, but I don't know what role you want him to play." Even though he was a friend to Cole, Mo maintained a regal attitude. But Paige guessed it matched the cop face Cole was surely wearing.

"I have Ahmed in the room with him now. I am hoping for good cop, bad cop. Hopefully with Ahmed standing there, he'll take option B by telling me everything for a deal."

Paige and Dani leaned closer when they didn't hear anything for a second.

"I am sorry, I cannot agree to that." Mo was really in royal mode. The definitive tone left nothing to question. Mo was calling the shots now. "He tried to kill Danielle, and for that he'll die in Rahmi. I am not going to allow him to live out his days in some comfortable American prison when he almost killed my fiancé, a future princess of Rahmi."

"You think I like this?" Cole ground out between clenched teeth. "Don't you think I want to kill the son of a bitch for what he's done to Paige?"

Dani and Paige shared a glance at each other that clearly filled Dani in on the relationship advancement she and Cole had gone through this afternoon.

"Then how can you possibly offer this man a deal?" Mo's voice was hard as Paige imagined the two of them standing face-to-face, glaring at each other.

"Because I want his testimony against the people who hired him. It's the only way to make sure they are locked up forever."

"What if there is another way?" Mo asked, his tone softer now.

"I am all ears if you have a way to get my testimony and have this guy get what he deserves."

"Offer him your deal after Ahmed talks to him. He should gladly leap at a chance to a plea deal. Offer him a really nice deal. Make sure you have him in solitary until his testimony, though. I don't want anything to happen to him."

"Mo, this doesn't make sense. I thought you wanted a harsher punishment."

"And I will get it. You make a deal on behalf of the FBI and local authorities. After his testimony, walk him out of court and hand him over to Ahmed."

"I can't do that. The United States can't just hand over a criminal to Rahmi, no matter how good our relations are with you."

"I am not talking about him disappearing. I am talking about a legal and already approved order of extradition." Paige could hear the triumph in Mo's voice.

"You have no grounds to extradition. He hasn't committed any crimes in Rahmi."

"According to the Rahmi-U.S. Treaty signed for oil imports, the United States agreed that any crimes against ambassadors, royalty, or any other dignitaries from Rahmi can be prosecuted in Rahmi court as long as a request for extradition has been submitted."

"Danielle is a United States citizen, she doesn't qualify." Poor Cole, he sounded so confused.

"There you are wrong. She qualifies as royalty and as a dignitary. The formal papers for our marriage have been accepted by my parents, the announcement has been made in Rahmi. As soon as those papers were signed and the announcement was made, she became one of the highest-ranking women in my country, and according to our laws, a citizen of Rahmi." Mo stopped and she could hear the smile on his lips. "As such, for the attempted assassination of the future princess of Rahmi, he is subject to extradition."

She heard Cole walk away and make a call she guessed to be to Phillip Salmond. She looked at Dani who silently shrugged her shoulders. They didn't know what to make of this situation. Frankly, Paige didn't know if she cared what happened to the assassin. But, she was pretty sure she would feel better the farther away from her he was.

"Salmond agreed to it. We are having the lawyers work up the papers now. They will be faxed to the ICU within the hour. Let's go see if our man has woken up."

Dani held out her good arm for Paige to grip as she tentatively took the couple of steps back to her wheelchair. She hated to admit it, but she was glad she had the wheelchair now. Her feet throbbed just sitting there. When she was standing, it felt like fire ripping her feet apart. Dani wheeled her back over to the gym equipment and went back to her physical therapy.

"Doesn't Mo have a gym at home?"

"Yes, but if I didn't get out of the house some, I would go crazy. I talked him into letting me do it here since there is an emergency button and doctors right down the hall," she said as she pointed to the multiple red emergency buttons stationed around the room.

Paige looked around the antiseptic room filled with a rainbow of flexi-bands, silver free weights, and a couple of machines that resembled torture racks. Dani eagerly pulled some handle on the torture rack and weights slid up and then down as she strained and grunted. She shook her head and was glad she didn't have to have therapy for her feet. She had always been a country girl. No gym needed. Why would a woman make those noises and faces in front of other people?

She had been lucky enough to stay in shape with riding, running around the farm, wrestling with her brothers, and shooting. As she got older, she walked five miles to town each day during the summer to see friends. She ran through the creek and helped harvest the crops. Then, as a young woman, she got Chuck. He was all the excuse she needed to go running through fields again.

"Are you, ugh, getting, ugh, ready for the, ugh, trial?" Dani grunted out during one of her reps.

"I guess. I honestly haven't thought about it. I know I will be called to testify, but I don't know much more than that. The prosecutor told me she'd give me a call on Monday to go over my testimony and the procedure of the trial. What about you?"

"Mo's attorney is helping me get ready. He's talked with the prosecutor and she's told him what she wants from me and what to expect from the defense. I must say, I can't wait for this to be over. I refused to start wedding plans until this is over."

"I am sure your mom isn't thrilled with that!"

"My mom understands. It's my dad who is going nuts. He has more parties lined up than I can count." Dani would have laughed if she had any breath left in her.

"How is the injury?" Paige asked, turning serious.

"Better. It still aches and the whole area feels tight, but I am told it's just part of the healing process. The more I work it out and stretch the area, the sooner I will get back to feeling normal."

"Have you talked to Kenna? I wonder how she's doing." Paige grabbed a pretty blue stretch band from the wall and tried to stretch it to no avail.

"She's doing great. Working on physical therapy, same as me, and trying to get Will to stop hovering. He's already brought back paint samples from the store to paint the nursery. Kenna just told him to put it all in the room. In three months, when they find out if it's a girl or a boy, she'll let him play painter." Paige laughed and thought of Will and Kenna. They were going to make such great parents. "Now that we have made the required small talk, I want to know about you and Cole."

"Huh?" Paige almost blushed. That was real smooth. She just wasn't prepared for that kind of question. Dani just raised an eyebrow and went back to the torture rack. "Well, I am not quite sure what will happen. He told me he loved me, but I have no idea how it will all work out once we get back to the real world."

"Real world? I didn't know you had left it."

"You know, when he goes back to Lexington and is no longer living with me." She fidgeted with the blue band again and threw it down after it snapped back and hit her in the face, much to Dani's amusement.

"Just don't overthink things. You all are perfect for each other and you'll both realize that if you just get out of your own way."

Paige rolled her chair back and forth and thought about what Dani said as she grunted out another set of exercises that were supposedly helping her. Maybe Dani was right. Maybe she should just go with the flow and see what happened next. "Enjoy the now" as her mother always told her when she started to worry about the future too much. With a new determination toward her future, Paige tried to relax and not think about Cole as Dani told her about their upcoming trip to Rahmi to prepare for the first wedding ceremony and then the subsequent wedding in Keeneston two days later.

Chapter Seventeen

Paige said goodbye to Dani and was wheeled away from the physical therapy room as soon as Cole got back. He didn't say anything and didn't fill them in on the interrogation. He just gave Dani a quick peck on the cheek, grabbed the handles to Paige's wheelchair, and started wheeling her to the car as if the checkered flag was waving at Bristol Speedway.

"Cole, what's going on?" Paige asked, gripping the armrests of the wheelchair as he took a corner on two wheels.

"Nothing. Why?" He asked, never taking his eyes off the finish line in the form of sliding doors.

"Oh, I don't know. Maybe because you're not telling me what happened and you're practically running for the door." Paige closed her eyes as he narrowly avoided hitting an old man making his way down the hall.

"It went fine. The son of a bitch is going to pay, but first I have to act like his buddy. He started talking the second I put a little piece of paper in front of him. Said we wouldn't go after him for the attempted murders of you, Kenna, and Dani. That really hurt, by the way, but he started talking so fast I was happy to just sit back and record it." He paused in his story as he weaved between a couple of gurneys being pushed by orderlies. "Seemed Judge Voggel was the sitting judge on his brother's case and promised to find a way to dismiss the charges if he cleaned up their little mess. But no worries, he'll be turned over to Rahmi as soon as he gives his testimony at trial."

Cole hurried through the double doors and ceremoniously dumped her into the passenger seat of Ahmed's Mercedes. Paige watched as he pushed the wheelchair back toward the ER doors and ran to the driver's door.

"Well, I am sure you are dying to get home." Cole peeled out of the hospital parking lot and made it back to Keeneston in record time.

Paige had to pry her hand from the "oh shit" bar above the window as Cole reached in and pulled her into his arms. He used his hip to close the door and practically ran to the shop door.

"I bet you're glad to be home. You can rest all night without any worries about men trying to kill you. With the medicine the doctor ordered, you won't even want to get out of bed until tomorrow afternoon."

Paige just stared at him, not knowing what to make of this sudden shift of character. Cole couldn't wait to get her inside. Oh, couldn't wait to get her in bed! Paige smiled and batted her eyelashes just slightly at Cole as he hurried Chuck outside and then back inside as soon as possible. How romantic! He couldn't wait to be with her! He carried her up the stairs to her apartment and reached her bedroom. He gently lowered her into the bed and pulled down the covers.

He stepped back and reached into his pocket for the condom. Wait. That wasn't a condom. That was a pill bottle. He shook out two pills and handed them to her before hurrying to the bathroom for a small cup of water.

"Here. Take these. They should help you get right to sleep." He shoved the cup into her hand, stood back, and waited for her to take them. She felt her mouth hanging open and shut it.

"Take these and you can sleep until the morning. By then, the worst of the swelling will be gone from your feet and then they'll just hurt as opposed to the pain you're feeling now."

"What's going on? I feel as if I am missing something."

"Nothing is going on." Cole stepped away from the bed and anxiously looked at his watch.

"Got somewhere to be?"

"No. Yes. Just have to get some things done and I am sure you want to get to bed after such a long day." Cole was practically hopping from one foot to the other.

"Fine. Have a good night." She swallowed the two pills, got a quick kiss on the forehead, and watched Cole rush out of her apartment and possibly out of her life.

Paige dreamt of running through the woods as fast as she could. She felt the pain of the thorns as they dug into her feet. If she could just make it to the creek, the fire in her feet would be extinguished. The cold water hit at her face, but she couldn't stop the fire licking at her feet.

She jolted awake at the second slobbery kiss and stared up at Chuck's face hanging over hers. His chocolate-brown eyes danced as his jowls billowed out.

"Hey, boy." Paige closed her eyes as Chuck gave her another slurp. She stretched her body and felt the tightness in her feet.

They were much tighter today, and they ached. But the fire was gone, just like Cole said it would be. She raised her hand and absently scratched Chuck's head as she thought about her life. Would Cole even call to check on her today?

She scratched behind Chuck's ears and heard the muted thumping of his tail against the down comforter. She ran her hand down his neck and stopped. She ran her hand around his neck and opened her eyes at the foreign object. A big red satin bow was tied to Chuck's neck. She followed the red ribbon around his neck and gasped.

A simple gold band with a solitaire diamond hung from the ribbon. Paige stared at its simple elegance and sighed. Damn dreams. It was not cool to mess with her like that. She closed her eyes and figured the meds were giving her strange dreams. She shook her head and told herself to wake up.

She slowly opened her eyes again and closed them quickly as Chuck gave her face another bath. Now she was definitely awake. She opened her eyes and felt her mouth fall open. The ribbon was still around Chuck's neck and the beautiful diamond ring was still dangling from his neck.

Her hand went to it and she felt the hardness of the diamond and the smoothness of the gold band. Yup, definitely real. She raised her eyes and scanned her room. They stopped at the man casually leaning against the door with a dozen red roses and a smile on his face.

Paige watched as Cole pushed away from the door and walked toward her. Could this be real? It felt real, but she thought he had walked out on her last night.

She wanted to say something, but nothing came out when she opened her mouth. So she just watched as Cole stopped beside the bed and went down to one knee.

"Paige, sweetheart, I love you with all my heart. Maybe it wasn't love at first sight, but then again, maybe it was. Maybe we made each other so mad because we knew, deep down, that we belong together. It just took our heads a little while to catch up with our hearts. I have loved our fights, I have loved our passion, and I have loved every moment I have had with you. There is nothing I want more than to have those moments with you for the rest of our lives. Will you marry me?"

Paige's first reaction was to leap out of bed and jump up and down. But, when she tried to move fast, her legs shrieked in opposition. She had to settle for throwing her arms around Cole's neck. She smiled into his neck as he held her tight against him.

"Yes, I will marry you. I love you, Cole Parker."

"I love you, too."

"Even enough to put up with my brothers?" She laughed as she felt tears of joy flowing down her cheek.

"I'll take the whole lot of them, even the world's ugliest dog." Chuck thumped his tail as Cole untied the ribbon. "Good work, boy." He slid the ring off the ribbon and into his hand.

Paige looked at it lying in the middle of his large palm. It looked so small, but it meant so much. He picked it up and slid it onto her finger. She held up her hand and watched as the diamond sparkled. She had loved the rings Dani and Kenna had gotten, but this one fit her. It wasn't small, it wasn't large, and it wasn't ornate. It was just simply beautiful.

She leaned forward and threw her arms around his neck and gave him a kiss he wouldn't forget. Her lips moved on his and she felt him open his mouth to her tongue. She ran her fingers through his black hair as she pulled him closer. As her breasts brushed against his chest, he moaned and ran his own hand through her hair. With their lips never parting, Cole pushed her down onto the bed and put all his love, worry, and relief into the kiss as his hands pulled her shirt over her head. She answered his kiss with one of her own as she unzipped his pants and shoved them down his hips.

"Cole?"

"Yes, sweetheart?" He reached around her and unclasped her bra, freeing her breasts.

"I think you should make love to your fiancée."

"Yes, ma'am."

Paige sat on Cole's lap in bed with a homemade milkshake in her hand to celebrate. She couldn't take her eyes off the ring. It was so perfect for her. It felt as if it was made for her.

"Cole, can I ask you something?"

"Sure, sweetheart."

"What happened last night? It was like you couldn't get away from me fast enough and then this." She wiggled her hand to watch the diamond flash.

"I was worried you would catch on to my plan. I knew the second I scooped you up into my arms in the field yesterday that I could never let you go again. I was frantic. The only thing I cared about was asking you to marry me. I couldn't wait to plan something romantic. I just had to ask you."

Paige rested her head again his chest and smiled. "It was perfect and very romantic."

"I'm glad. I thought about it as I drove to Tennessee last night."

"Tennessee?"

"Yeah." He blushed slightly as if he was embarrassed. "I had to get the ring. It's tradition in my family for the eldest son to have his mother's ring. The ring has been passed down for six generations."

"Really? But what about your mother?" His mother must be heartbroken to lose her ring.

"I wouldn't worry about my mother. The women started another tradition. When it came time to relinquish the ring, they get a new, bigger one. Something about putting in the time and deserving it!"

"So, for six generations, this very ring has been passed down?"

"Yup. It belonged to my great-great-great-great-grandfather. It's around one hundred fifty years old. My ancestor was an English carpenter and bought this ring before heading to America right after the Civil War. He wanted a new life and knew America needed a lot of hard-working men after losing so many in the war. So, he bought the ring and carried it with him across the ocean. He had heard that the area surrounding Murfreesboro had been annihilated by the war. The area was in ruin and men were in short order. Being in his late thirties and still unmarried, he figured his odds were pretty good. Once he landed in America, he headed to Murfreesboro. He was instantly hired to rebuild the Methodist Church. While working there, he met the preacher's daughter and fell in love.

"They had eight children. When the eldest son came home from a dance and told his mother he had met a girl he wanted to marry, she took off her ring and handed it to him. Told him it had brought her and his father so much good luck she wanted to pass it on to him. My great-great-great-grandfather and his wife had six children before passing the ring on. The ring was passed on through the generations until now."

"So, what happens if we don't have a boy?"

"I wouldn't worry about it. Between your family and mine, I think it's in the genes." Cole stopped and held her hand in his, looking at the ring on her finger. "So, is this better than the vacuum?"

Paige laughed and leaned her head back to give him a kiss. "Let me just show you how much better!"

Chapter Eighteen

Paige woke up with a smile. They had spent yesterday in bed together. They watched movies, ate ice cream, drank champagne, and made love all afternoon. She opened her eyes and rolled over to look at the clock. Nine-thirty! Oh crap, she had to get moving. After this weekend, today would be the busiest day of the year. Everyone would be stopping in to hear about the Davies Shoot-Out as the deputies had been calling it.

Paige swung her legs over the side of the bed and gingerly tried to put some weight on them. It hurt, but not enough to stop her from slowly making her way to the bathroom for a nice, hot shower.

She opened the shower door and saw Cole standing there with his arms crossed over his chest and his cop face on.

"What do you think you are doing?" Cole asked.

Paige gave him a quick look and wondered if this was a trick question. She looked down at her naked self and back up to Cole's glare. "Um, I am pretty sure I was taking a shower."

"They told you not to get the stitches wet for three days. You need to get back to bed. Now."

Oh, well that did it. Paige wiggled her toes in the trash bags that she had put on to keep her feet dry and gave him a look that told him to shove it.

"I have a store to run, a store that will have one of its most profitable business days of the year, thanks to the nosy people of my town. However, I have to say, at least they buy something when they come in to gossip. And just because this beautiful, amazing ring is on my finger and just because I love you to pieces, does not mean you get to order me around, thank you very much." Paige reached past him and grabbed the towel from the rack and started to dry off.

"I will run the store. You get back into bed and rest those feet. Paige, I say this because I love you and I don't like to see you hurting."

Oh, sneaky. There was no way she could stay mad at him for that. "I'll make you a deal. If you will help me with the store today, then I will stay off my feet. However, I insist you set me up downstairs."

"Deal."

Paige sat in a chair with her feet up behind the counter. After a call was placed to Betty Jo for emergency support, Paige had managed to get the store opened just thirty minutes late. Cole stocked shelves, Betty Jo worked on sales, and Paige rang up the purchases.

"OOOHHH! Here she is! The lovely bride-to-be!" The Rose sisters sang as they came through the door.

Paige looked around and then realized they were talking to her. They couldn't be, though. She hadn't told anyone. Cole had called her parents and invited the whole family over for dinner. However, her mom had pointed out the problems with the whole family eating at her place and had instead invited them over to her house. She was going to tell her family at dinner tonight.

"Me?"

"Of course you, silly. Show us the ring!" Miss Lily grabbed her hand and turned the diamond ring up.

"How do you all know? I haven't told anyone." Paige tried to get them to keep their voice down, but they blatantly ignored the hint.

"Oh honey, *everyone* knows," Miss Daisy told her. Paige looked up to the packed house and saw everyone nod and smile.

"Your mom has been calling everyone. You're the first one in the family to get married. She couldn't be happier," Miss Violet piped in.

"I even put ten dollars on May 23rd."

Paige turned and stared at Mrs. Wyatt and her white face and bright red lipstick. "What?" Maybe Mrs. Wyatt was confused and thought they were talking about something else.

"For the baby pool. I'm betting on a quick wedding." She winked, which was lost under the wide brim of her hat.

"Baby pool?" Paige stammered.

"Sure, over at the cafe. They have a baby pool going." Paige shot her eyes over to the Rose sisters who were suddenly very interested in the jewelry on the other side of the store. Just as guiltily, Cole came over taking an interest in the countertop.

"Um, it's also kind of my fault."

"You didn't tell them when you called, did you?"

"Not when I called this morning, no."

"I hear a 'but' coming."

"But, your brother Pierce needs to have his butt kicked." Paige just stared him down as Cole started to fidget with the pins for sale. "Well, as soon as I got back from Tennessee, I guess it was around five-thirty in the morning. I stopped by your parents' house to talk to your dad.

"While I was out on the porch with your dad asking his permission to marry you, Pierce woke up your mom and called all your brothers. Within ten minutes, your mom, Miles, Marshall, Cade, Pierce, and even Cy via videoconference on the laptop, were all out on the porch with me. They asked me how much money I make, about my job security, and where we'll live. It was the toughest interrogation I have seen." Cole reached across the counter and tweaked her nose. "You're worth it, though."

Paige smiled and held out her arms. Cole came around the counter and hugged her as the older women came back around the counter cooing. Could life get any better?

"Aw, how cute, the shop owner is marrying the stock boy." Kandi sashayed into the shop. She sure did have great timing. It was like some homing device. She had to ruin a good day.

Paige tried to stand up, but Cole placed a gentle hand on her shoulder. Paige looked up at him and saw his silver eyes dance and a smile reach from ear to ear.

"You mean you don't know who I am, Cindy?"

Paige stifled a laugh that Miss Lily didn't feel the need to muffle. Paige looked around the shop and saw all the customers slowly move toward the counter to be able to hear and see the action better.

"It's Kandi, you silly goose. And of course I know who you are. You are the clerk who slept his way to the top." Kandi laughed at her own joke. "My, you work fast!" She gave him a wink as the collective crowd gasped. Cole just laughed.

"How are you the only person in town who doesn't know who Cole is?" Paige asked. A smile began to creep across her lips. Maybe Kandi wouldn't ruin her day after all.

"I just said I know him." Kandi put her hands on her hips and stuck out her floatation devices. She was smiling as if she just won the lottery. Oh, Paige was going to have fun with this.

"No, I mean, how are you the only person in town that doesn't know that Cole is a Special Agent for the FBI?" Paige sat back in her chair and grabbed Cole's hand.

"FBI?" Kandi sputtered.

"Actually, sweetheart, I have been meaning to tell you something. Since bringing down the ring of corruption in Congress and the judicial system, and catching an internationally wanted assassin with your wonderful help, the Director of the FBI has made me the Special Agent in Charge of the Lexington Office."

Congratulations filled the room as Kandi made her departure unnoticed. Kandi didn't matter anymore. As Paige reached up and brought his lips to hers, she realized high school was finally over and she had a new life to start with a man she loved.

After a long celebration at her parents' home, they drove back to her place for another private celebration. They couldn't keep their hands off each other. After making love again, she laid her head on his bare chest. She ran her hand over his flat stomach and through the light sprinkling of dark chest hair. She listened to the strong rhythm of his heartbeat as she explored his chest.

"Cole, you mentioned that my parents asked about our plans for the future." She heard the rumble in his chest of agreement and continued. "So, I was wondering, what did you tell them?" They had not discussed the future past getting engaged. She guessed it was irresponsible, but the feeling of peace and contentment told her it was okay.

"Well, with my promotion, I will be running the office. I will be in the field less, but on call more. I hope you don't mind."

"Not at all. I feel much better having you answer the phone as opposed to going into the field."

"I am glad. It also comes with a nice pay raise. A pay raise that's nice enough to buy the house that's for sale around the corner. The one with the large fenced yard perfect for Chuck and as many kids as possible."

"That sounds like a dream come true," Paige sighed as she snuggled closer.

"I can pinch you to see if you wake up." Cole laughed as he pinched her bottom.

She smacked his hand away and laughed. "If this is a dream, then I don't want to ever wake up," Paige murmured as Cole ran his hand slowly up and down her back.

"Sweetheart, we have the rest of our lives to dream. But right now, I want you awake for what I am going to do to you." Cole grinned before kissing her again and she decided dreaming was overrated compared to her new life with Cole. Maybe her mother was right after all!

Chapter Nineteen

One Month Later...

Paige reached over to her left and linked her hand with Dani's. Dani similarly linked her other hand with Kenna. They each squeezed each other's hands in a sign of support.

"You girls ready for this?" Kenna asked as she looked at her best friends.

"You bet your ass, girl," Dani told her, reading Paige's mind.

Paige, Dani, and Kenna looked up the marble stairs at the large gray stone building in front of them. Cars honked and people shoved them as they walked hurriedly by. The end-of-August air was smothering. The United States Courthouse loomed over them like a medieval castle.

Kenna couldn't believe this used to be her home. Now all she wanted to do was get back to Kentucky and watch the UK vs. UL football game and pick out baby names. She looked at Dani and could tell by the expression on her face that she felt the same way. New York City was no longer their home. But they had one more thing to do before leaving the city behind.

Kenna felt Will come up and take her left hand in his. He placed it in the crook of his arm and smiled down on her. She dropped Dani's hand and placed her other hand on her small baby bump. It seemed like a lifetime ago when she and Dani ran from this city. Now it was about closure. Now it was about justice.

As soon as Dani felt Kenna pull her hand away, it was replaced by the strong hold of her fiancé who had stepped up next to her. She was ready to do this, with or without the support of Mo and her friends. But it sure did help to have them here.

Cole slipped his arm around Paige's shoulder and pulled her against him. With a wink, he kissed her forehead. She looked down the line at the prosecutor's star witnesses and hoped their motion to be allowed in the courtroom during trial would be granted. The defense had asked that they be excluded, but Kenna had made sure the prosecutor filed a motion to allow them to be there.

"Well, let's get this over with. Football season starts this weekend," Will joked.

"And we have a wedding shower in Italy," Mo told the others.

"And we have a wedding to plan," Cole informed them.

The girls shook their heads and laughed. Their men knew how to ease the tension. They started up the first set of stairs when Will's cell phone rang. He answered it and held up his hand to stop everyone. He pushed a button on his phone and held it out for everyone to hear.

"Okay, go ahead. We're all here," Will spoke into the phone.

"Hello? Can you hear us? Are ya'll there?" Miss Lily's Southern voice sounded like an angel against the harsh New Yorkers' accent they had listened to the past couple of days.

"Hush a minute and let them answer you, Lily Rae."

"I was doing just that when you opened your mouth, Daisy Mae."

"Bless your hearts, girls, shut up a minute so they can hear us," Miss Violet said in the background. Kenna rolled her eyes, Dani laughed out loud, and Paige felt the peace and warmth of home float through the phone to envelop her.

"We're here!" Will shouted into the phone.

"We hear you, William. No need to shout. We wanted to call and wish our girls luck. We called the church and sent out a prayer tree. You all have the support of the town," Miss Lily told them.

"Hurry home, we miss you already!" Miss Violet shouted.

"And we're already making a pitcher of our special tea for when you get home." There was a pause before Miss Daisy continued, "And some regular boring lemonade for those of you in the family way."

"Thank you, Miss Daisy!" Kenna, Dani and Paige each said in unison.

"Thanks for thinking of us. We'll be home as soon as we can," Kenna told them before Will took the phone off speaker.

Paige looked over and saw the shimmer in Kenna's eyes. "Damn pregnancy hormones."

"Yeah, they work both ways, though. Our child support payments have never been better. No parent wants to come into court and face a hormonal attorney for failure to pay child support. We're actually getting kinda bored," Dani joked.

The group quieted and looked back up at the courthouse.

"Let's do it, girls." Paige looked to each of her friends, now closer than sisters, as they headed into the deep hallows of the courthouse surrounded by Ahmed, Rahmi soldiers, and U.S. marshals.

The group was seated in a conference hall near the U.S. Attorney's Office. In the first chair was the U.S. Attorney for the region. He was tall and thin with salt-and-pepper hair sharply cut. His glasses matched his standard black suit. Seated in the second chair was the woman who had handled the grand jury. Her mousy brown hair was clipped back and she too had on a black suit. Paige glanced at Kenna's French twist and black suit.

"I know, I know, we look like funeral directors. It is just such an ingrained habit that I couldn't break it now." Paige smiled at her and noticed the woman ADA looked down at her black suit as if just noticing for the first time they were all dressed alike.

"So, we won the Motion for Sequestration because of victims' rights. Victims of Crimes have pushed for victims' rights in the court procedures. In the old days, it was standard for all witnesses to be kept out of the courtroom except to testify. Well, the new victims' rights state that victims of a crime should be afforded every opportunity to confront the accused. As long as a legitimate reason is not given for exclusion, the new thought is victims have every right to be present through all the proceedings.

"The defense tried to exclude you all by saying testimony from one of you would affect testimony from the others. Essentially, you would taint each other. However, since you have each submitted very thorough affidavits and McKenna has testified in person before the grand jury, and Danielle had provided a taped statement, the court allowed you all to be present through the trial.

"We have already selected our jury. Opening statements will be made and then McKenna will be called to testify. After McKenna, it will be Danielle, then Agent Parker, Paige, our friendly assassin, and finally Director Salmond. I hope to finish with our case at the end of the week. The defense could take up to two weeks. This is a marathon, not a sprint. Do not lose hope. Do not roll your eyes. Do not get upset. Stay calm, collected, graceful, and strong. Now, are you ready to go?"

Kenna felt the familiar rush as she walked into the large courtroom. A feeling of confidence washed over her as she slipped into attorney mode. It was hard for her to realize she wasn't here to argue a case. She was the case. She smiled up at Lady Justice and knew everything would be alright.

Dani followed Kenna's sure stride and blinked at all the cameras aimed at them. This was the media event of the century. How did Kenna do it? Her face was solemn and confident, and she didn't even break a sweat. Dani couldn't do that, though. She needed support. As if reading her mind, Mo's hand came to rest gently on her back as he led her through the crowd and to the bench behind the prosecutor's table. She briefly closed her eyes and took a deep breath.

Paige stopped at the door and looked in awe at the courtroom. Everything was so elaborate and big. The bench stood high above the room so the judge could survey his domain. Dark mahogany paneling covered the walls as large chandeliers hung down lighting the room, a room packed with media. All their cameras were now pointed at her. She slowly made her way past them with Cole's hand in hers. She was sure he could feel her trembling since he gave her hand a supportive squeeze. She passed the families of the defendants and couldn't stop from giving them a sympathetic smile. She slid into her seat and waited for the wheels of justice to turn.

"All rise! The United States Court of the Southern District of New York, the Honorable Judge Guillentino presiding, is now in session," the bailiff announced. The courtroom quieted as the short old judge made his way to the bench.

"Please be seated and come to order. Are you prepared for your opening statements?" The judge asked.

When both attorneys said "Yes, Your Honor," the judge pulled out a notepad and put on a pair of wire-rimmed glasses.

"Proceed."

Paige leaned back and became engrossed in the opening statements. Hours passed as the attorneys wove their tales of guilt and innocence, of facts and fiction, and of evidence or the lack thereof.

"The prosecution may call its first witness," the judge told U.S. Attorney.

"The prosecution calls McKenna Mason Ashton to the stand."

Kenna stood as her name was called. Will squeezed her hand before letting go. She straightened her jacket over her unborn child and found a type of strength she never knew existed. As she walked past the defense table, her heels clicked on the stone floor and she turned to look the men right in the eyes. She wanted them to know she was not backing down. Instead she was taking them down.

She walked in front of the defense table and stopped in front of the step leading up to the witness stand. She turned and waited for the bailiff to swear her in. She kept her eyes on the defense table and smothered a grin when Bob Greendale squirmed in his chair. She had some things she wanted to say. She had a family to protect… her husband, her unborn child, and her sisters. Nothing, and no one, was going to stand in her way of convicting these assholes. If she couldn't be the one prosecuting them, then she'd do something even better. She'd provide the testimony to put them in jail for the rest of their lives.

"Please raise your right hand. Do you swear to tell the truth, the whole truth, and nothing but the truth, so help you God?"

"I do."

Epilogue

Keeneston Journal
February 9th

- Mr. and Mrs. Will Ashton proudly announce the birth of their healthy baby girl, Sienna Danielle Paige Ashton. She was born February 7th at 11:15 at night.

- His Royal Highness Mohtadi Ali Rahman and Her Royal Highness Danielle Ali Rahman, AKA Mo and Dani, have returned from their honeymoon after the wedding of the century. Residents are still recovering from the President of the United States of America's stay in Keeneston.

- Miss Lily Rae Rose has announced the Man O' War room is now called the Presidential Suite after the President slept there while attending the wedding two months ago.

- Mr. Cole Parker and Miss Paige Davies announce that they will be holding their wedding this spring out at the Davies Farm. The wedding will be held May 13th.

- Following the Royal Wedding, Miss Paige Davies has been commissioned to supply Derby hats for both the First Lady of the United States and the First Lady of France after they saw one of her hats featured in *Vogue*.

- In related news, all bets placed in the Cole and Paige baby pool for a delivery date prior to October, have been disqualified. Dates are now open for the new year. Bets are $5 per date. See Miss Daisy Mae Rose or Miss Violet Fae Rose for more information.

- Our very own Deputy Noodle won first place in the Eighth Annual Kentucky Noodling Contest by catching a catfish weighing in at sixty-three pounds!

- Pam Gilbert of the PTA has announced a bake sale to support the baseball team. It will be held at the Keeneston Farmer's Market from 9 to12 this Saturday.

- Bob Greendale, Dick LeMaster, Gene Pottinger, Brian Voggel, and Jarred Felting were sentenced to life imprisonment yesterday in New York City. Good riddance.

- Adaline Brunston won first prize at this year's Confederate Daughters' Bake Off to Support the Troops. Her winning pie will be featured at the Blossom Cafe all this week.

- Saint Francis announces that they will host a fish fry at the Church from 5 to 8 this Friday. Everyone is invited for dinner and live music. See John Wolfe for more information.

Other Books by Kathleen Brooks

Bluegrass Brothers Series Continues!

The fifth and final book in the Bluegrass Brothers Series will be out in the Fall of 2013. Be sure to like me on Facebook (facebook.com/KathleenBrooksAuthor) or follow my Blog (www.kathleen-brooks.blogspot.com) to get updates on the release date!

> *The mysterious Cy Davies is coming home. He's not coming alone either. Having rescued Gemma Perry, a sassy investigative reporter for a gossip magazine, he takes her to the one place he knows he can keep her safe. Keeneston.*
>
> *Gemma Perry was having a bad week. Now she was in a small town where gossip was a currency. She should fit right in, except for the fact that she unwillingly holds the secret to bring down an internationally wanted man who is sparing no expense to keep those secrets safe.*

And I just couldn't leave Keeneston without a proper finale. Ahmed will be getting a book too! Ahmed's book is scheduled for release in early 2014. More details will come soon.

★　　★　　★

Bluegrass Series

Bluegrass State of Mind

McKenna Mason, a New York City attorney with a love of all things Prada, is on the run from a group of powerful, dangerous men. McKenna turns to a teenage crush, Will Ashton, for help in starting a new life in beautiful horse country. She finds that Will is now a handsome, successful race horse farm owner. As the old flame is ignited, complications are aplenty in the form of a nasty ex-wife, an ex-boyfriend intent on killing her, and a feisty race horse who refuses to race without a kiss. Can Will and McKenna cross the finish line together, and more importantly, alive?

Risky Shot

Danielle De Luca, an ex-beauty queen who is not at all what she seems, leaves the streets of New York after tracking the criminals out to destroy her. She travels to Keeneston, Kentucky, to make her final stand by the side of her best friend McKenna Mason. While in Keeneston, Danielle meets the quiet and mysterious Mohtadi Ali Rahman, a modern day prince. Can Mo protect Dani from the group of powerful men in New York? Or will Dani save the prince from his rigid, loveless destiny?

Dead Heat

In the third book of the Bluegrass Series, Paige Davies finds her world turned upside down as she becomes involved in her best friend's nightmare. The strong-willed Paige doesn't know which is worse: someone trying to kill her, or losing her dog to the man she loves to hate.

FBI Agent Cole Parker can't decide whether he should strangle or kiss this infuriating woman of his dreams. As he works the case of his career, he finds that love can be tougher than bringing down some of the most powerful men in America.

Bluegrass Brothers Series

Bluegrass Undercover

Cade Davies had too much on his plate to pay attention to newest resident of Keeneston. He was too busy avoiding the Davies Brothers marriage trap set by half the town. But when a curvy redhead lands in Keeneston, the retired Army Ranger finds himself drawn to her. These feelings are only fueled by her apparent indifference and lack of faith in his ability to defend himself.

DEA Agent Annie Blake was undercover to bust a drug ring hiding in the adorable Southern town that preyed on high school athletes. She had thought to keep her head down and listen to the local gossip to find the maker of this deadly drug. What Annie didn't count on was becoming the local gossip. With marriage bets being placed, and an entire town aiming to win the pot, Annie looks to Cade for help in bringing down the drug ring before another kid is killed. But can she deal with the feelings that follow?

Rising Storm

Katelyn Jacks was used to being front and center as a model. But she never had to confront the Keeneston Grapevine! After retiring from the runway and returning to town to open a new animal clinic, Katelyn found that her life in the public eye was anything but over. While working hard to establish herself as the new veterinarian in town, Katelyn finds her life uprooted by a storm of love, gossip, and a vicious group of criminals.

Marshall Davies is the new Sheriff in Keeneston. He is also right at the top of the town's most eligible bachelor list. His affinity for teasing the hot new veterinarian in town has led to a rush of emotions that he wasn't ready for. Marshall finds his easy days of breaking up fights at the local PTA meetings are over when he and Katelyn discover that a dog-fighting ring has stormed into their normally idyllic town. As their love struggles to break through, they must battle to save the lives of the dogs and each other.

Secret Santa, A Bluegrass Series Novella

It wouldn't be Christmas in Keeneston without a party! Everyone's invited, even Santa...

Kenna's court docket is full, Dani's hiding from her in-laws, Paige and Annie are about to burst from pregnancy, and Marshall is breaking up fights at the PTA Christmas Concert. The sweet potato casserole is made, the ham and biscuits are on the table, and men are losing their shirts—and not because of bets placed with the Rose Sisters! All the while, the entire town is wondering one thing: who is the Secret Santa that showed up with special gifts for everyone?

Acquiring Trouble

As a natural born leader, Miles Davies accomplishes anything he puts his mind to. Upon returning home from his special forces duties, he has become the strong foundation of the Davies family and his company. But that strong foundation is about to get rocked in a big way by the one woman that always left him fascinated and infuriated.

Keeneston's notorious bad girl is back! Morgan Hamilton's life ended and began on her high school graduation night when she left Keeneston with no plan to ever return. As a self-made businesswoman, Morgan is always looking for her next victory. Little did she know that next victory would involve acquiring the company that belonged to the one man she always wanted for herself.

With their careers and lives on the line, will Miles and Morgan choose love or ambition?

Relentless Pursuit

Pierce Davies watched as his older siblings fell in love – something this bachelor was not ready for. After all, he was now the most eligible man in all of Keeneston! Though Pierce enjoys the playboy lifestyle, his life is his work and that hard work is set to pay off big time with the unveiling of a big secret. However, this work hard, play hard attitude may have also landed him in hot water as he finds himself arrested for a brutal murder with all evidence pointing to him.

Tammy Fields has been suffering from the crush to end all crushes. But her flirtations have fallen short as Pierce Davies always ended up in the arms of a Keeneston Belle. Having waited long enough, Tammy decides now is the time to grow up and move on. She has a good job as a paralegal and a hot new boyfriend. But everything changes quickly when Pierce is arrested and Tammy is called upon to help with his case. While working closely with Pierce to prove his innocence, she realizes her crush is something far more meaningful as she risks everything to save him.

Will they finally find love or will the increasing danger prevent their happily ever after?

Make sure you don't miss each new book as they are published. Sign up email notification of all new releases at http://www.Kathleen-Brooks.com.

About the Author

Kathleen Brooks has garnered attention for her debut novel, Bluegrass State of Mind, as a new voice in romance with a warm Southern feel. Her books feature quirky, small town characters you'll feel like you've known forever, romance, humor, and mystery all mixed into one perfect glass of sweet tea.

Kathleen is an animal lover who supports rescue organizations and other non-profit organizations whose goals are to protect and save our four-legged family members.

Kathleen lives in Central Kentucky with her husband, daughter, two dogs, and a cat who thinks he's a dog. She loves to hear from readers and can be reached at Kathleen@Kathleen-Brooks.com.

Check out the Kathleen Brooks's Website, www.Kathleen-Brooks.com for updates on in the Bluegrass Series. You can also "Like" Kathleen on Facebook (facebook.com/KathleenBrooksAuthor) and follow her on Twitter @BluegrassBrooks.

Special Thank You!

To the fans that have written me and wanted more of Keeneston, I have loved writing this trilogy and am excited about my future projects. Thank you for your support and kind words.

CPSIA information can be obtained
at www.ICGtesting.com
Printed in the USA
LVHW031006120319
610345LV00003B/157/P